BATSHIT

Delhi girl, cat lady and zombie-novel-aficionado **Kritika Kapoor** currently lives in Pune and works as Assistant Editor for *Delhi Times*, *Times of India*. During her over a decade-long career at *TOI*, which includes a four-year stint as the editor of *Goa Times*, she has written about topics ranging from art and literature to cinema and pop culture.

Batshit is her first novel.

BATSHIT

KRITIKA
KAPOOR

PAN

First published in 2023 by Pan
an imprint of Pan Macmillan Publishing India Private Limited
707 Kailash Building
26 K. G. Marg, Delhi 110001
www.panmacmillan.co.in

Pan Macmillan, The Smithson, 6 Briset Street, London EC1M 5NR
Associated companies throughout the world
www.panmacmillan.com

ISBN 978-93-95624-47-3

This is a work of fiction. Names, characters, businesses, organizations, places, events, and incidents either are the product of the author's imagination or are used fictitiously. Any resemblance to actual persons, living or dead, events, or locales is entirely coincidental.

1 3 5 7 9 8 6 4 2

Typeset in Bembo Std by SÜRYA, New Delhi
Printed and bound in India by Replika Press Pvt. Ltd.

For Mom, Dad
and thirteen-year-old Kritika

1

ONE WEEK TO THE WEDDING

Raghav

He barely recognizes the laughter coming out of the kitchen. It doesn't fit in with the usual morning cacophony of unruly birds screaming in the trees, the vegetable vendor's off-key *raag* listing the day's inventory, the dull thud of the knife slicing into tomatoes, onions and chicken on the cutting board, and the sharp hiss and piercing whistles of the pressure cooker.

No. Today, Pia's laughter gurgles and bubbles over all the usual din, and as he walks towards her, he picks up on the rapid, almost manic tempo of her speech even though he can't understand what she's saying. He presumes she's sitting at the dining table, talking to someone on her cellphone. Through the doorway, he only catches a glimpse of her bare feet, the toes dancing animatedly to her sing-song voice. He finds himself getting hard at this sight and the sound of her.

He inches closer slowly, until he can see a hint of her ankles. The curve of her calves.

Closer inspection reveals her faintly scarred knees, and her bare thighs, to the point where her t-shirt is no longer skimming them.

When he steps over the wet rag on the floor, he skids and trips over the bucket of soap water next to it.

Her toes stop dancing.

Her voice drops to a muffled whisper, followed by a silence that amplifies the birds' shrill screeches, the pressure cooker's threatening whistle and the *sabziwala*'s hideous classical ode to his stock of brinjals and carrots.

When Raghav finally enters the kitchen, he sees the same old Pia leaning against the counter and fussing over the chicken.

Quiet, languid and almost bovine in both form and movement – this Pia he finds increasingly hard to sexualize as the days go by.

Her plump frame is draped in a faded grey t-shirt that once belonged to him. She borrowed it on the first night she slept over at his place and it has been her favourite ever since. It's now torn, tattered and falling apart at the seams, and he doubts she's ever changed out of it in the two years they've been dating. Though she once used to swim in it, the fabric clings softly to her new curves. Her wild, curly, unwashed mane is piled up in a haphazard knot held together by a pen. It threatens to fall apart any second, as she stares intently at a soggy printout lying next to the stove.

'Good morning,' he says softly. She turns around. As he stares into her now-round face, with its comically large features – large, mud-coloured eyes, a wide nose and a gaping Julia Roberts smile – he realizes he's gone soft.

Still, he goes behind her and, circling her waist with his arms, drops a kiss on her nape. 'Who was that?' He realizes he's not particularly interested in her response.

'A friend,' she replies, in an equally off-handed tone, her hands folding over his on her stomach with the same absent-mindedness.

Peering over her shoulder, he notices the wet white sheet currently arresting her attention. The first line, written in blotchy ink, reads:

Keto Phase 1: Moroccan Chicken. 360 calories.

'Chai?' she asks.

But he's already picked up his car keys.

On his way out, he spots her cellphone on the drawing room sofa. For a split second, he wonders if Pia has a landline before the aux cord in his car sputters to life and the thumping Progressive beats take over.

Pia

She does not change out of the t-shirt she has been wearing all weekend to take a shower and then go to work, as she is supposed to. And she ignores her cellphone, which has been buzzing all morning, still lying on the couch, with 'mom' flashing angrily across the screen.

Instead, the sound of Raghav's car skidding through the driveway gravel, and the first beep of the horn as he exits the front gate and onto the main road, is her cue to grab an ashtray from her living room and a mangled pack of Marlboros from her bag, and head to the storeroom at the far end of the house.

She crosses the large drawing room with blue walls, wooden floors and grey sofas into the corridor leading to two bedrooms – both painted black and white – with sprawling king-sized beds that Pia lays across almost every night by herself, picking one depending on her mood. It's a spacious apartment that was designed tastefully by her mother, but Pia managed to strip it off any or all character in the last two years. The flat looks like it hasn't seen an inhabitant in years. The walls are bare, as are the tables and desks, save for unwanted items such as pens without caps, or books she never intends to finish. The showpieces collect dust, the clothes lie in forgotten piles, the plants droop lifelessly – she walks past all of them unmindfully, finally reaching the door to the third bedroom.

It's been a few months since she's been on the other side. The lock is brown and rusted, and she has to twist and jiggle the key for several minutes while leaning her entire body weight into the door for it to finally give. Inside, the room smells of dust. Today, as the tall paint-splattered and cobwebbed walls welcome her to the only part of this house that has ever felt like home, she is drawn to the abandoned ghost town of easels and canvases covered in white sheets.

Pia rips a sheet off one canvas, brushes away the cobwebs and starts working with the new set of oil paints she'd picked up in a spurt of inspiration the day before.

She goes through a pack of cigarettes, three cups of black coffee, and more than half the morning, painting her frenzied thoughts.

There's something about all that nicotine and caffeine

rushing through her system at the same time that gives her an illusion of control while also agitating and fraying her nerves enough to spill the contents of her brain and heart directly onto the huge expanse of white blankness in front of her.

With violent cigarette puffs and brush strokes, she tries to capture and tame her thoughts – 1970s' Bollywood movie poster style, while drenching herself in red, blue and yellow in the process.

She draws herself doe-eyed and with beehive hair, her expression desperate and wane, as she addresses Raghav in her head: '*You know my dad has high blood pressure. You know all he wants is to see me married and maybe a grandchild. You know I'm almost goddamn thirty years old now! I mean, what are we even waiting for? The last of my eggs to die?*'

She chooses an unnecessarily flashy, bright red shirt for Raghav, with a blue scarf tied around his neck. The shirt almost matches the colour of his face, as he stands before her, looking like an Angry Young Man.

You're twenty-seven, for God's sake. Both your father and your eggs have another ten years at least. Stop pressuring me into a decision I am not ready for, she imagines him snapping at her.

So, basically – Ila, her friend from school, interjects – *You're settling for him.*

Pia draws her in a vampy get-up, mid-cabaret, *a la* Helen.

For her mother, she chooses the only Bollywood mother template she knows. She meshes her features with Nirupama Roy's trademark greying hair, white sari and bindi (that her own mother in crisp Fabindia salwar kameezes – her hair blow-dried and still black, with brown and honey highlights – would scoff at).

He treats you well. He takes care of you. How is that settling? Pia imagines her saying, with a sad violin wailing in the background.

She then takes a step back, tired and filthy from the paint, sweat and tears.

But the voices don't leave.

There are other, better reasons to get married, Ila's attitude is getting more condescending, assuming that sense of superiority and authority that Pia both despised and obeyed back then.

Those reasons can't be your father's fucking blood pressure, or your dying eggs, Raghav sounds both angry and helpless.

Then what should they be … Love? Her mother's sarcasm is a punch to her gut.

They all glare at her from the canvas. She can feel herself being cut off from the conversation once more.

Pia sighs and covers their disapproving, still-wet faces with the white sheet, stubbing the end of her cigarette and gulping down the last of her coffee.

2

SIX DAYS TO THE WEDDING

Kabir

He digs the 'hot mess' vibe Pia's always got going on.

She breezes into office three hours late, as usual – smelling of lemons and Delhi winters, with a hint of smoke. Her kajal no longer lines her lower lids like it should, but is smudged panda-style under her eyes in a way that you'd think would be unattractive, except it's not. Her clothing's more subterfuge than style; it's always a variation of a baggy black sweatshirt, paired with the same baggy blue jeans. It makes him wonder what she's hiding underneath. He notices how she's tried taming her curly hair into some kind of a half-bun today. As she marches down the long corridor in his direction, it flops around like a miserable creature restrained against its will.

Yup, Kabir realizes, he *totally* digs Pia.

Zara, their boss, stops her midway. 'Wasn't your copy on that Bollywood actress' wedding at Barwara Fort due, like, a week ago?'

At twenty-eight, Zara is on the *Forbes* '30 Under 30' list for her entrepreneurial skills and her brainchild, TalkOfTheTown, a website dedicated to food, fashion and lifestyle in Delhi. A Columbia graduate, she founded the company on her own, from the bedroom of her family's South Ex *kothi.* Since then, it has expanded to a fourteen-person team, operating out of a vintage bungalow-turned-office in GK-2, which also houses a fitness start-up and a rent-an-office space. While the outside of the bungalow has been preserved to look like a crumbling remnant of ancient beauty, the insides couldn't have been more surrealistically millennial – a high ceiling, yellow walls, one side with red bean bags littered across the floor, a foosball table and a makeshift cafe; and the other, tiny cubicles for each of the thirteen employees.

Zara, who sits in a cabin with all-glass doors overlooking her one-floor empire, is now in the process of launching new operations in other Indian metros.

Mean, hot, skinny and 5 feet 11 inches tall, Zara cuts an intimidating figure in her boyfriend jeans and black tee that reads 'Boss Bitch', but Pia, who they all joke is employee-most-likely-to-flip-out-and-shoot-the-entire-office-one-day, is a worthy opponent. Kabir believes it's her blank face, heavy kajal and silence that lends her such an elusive (and office shooter-type) aura. She's been here for almost a year, and none of the other employees recall ever having a conversation with her.

Pia mumbles something about it being on the way, which Zara has no choice but to accept as a reasonable excuse. 'Just have it in my inbox by tomorrow,' Zara sighs, asking no one in particular, 'I seriously thought that chick could afford Tuscany, though. Wasn't her fiancé the son of a liquor baron?'

The scent of lemon, Delhi winter, and smoke wafts past Kabir as Pia walks by without looking at him and settles into her seat two desks away. Then she drops her bag to the floor, switches on her laptop and puts on the ginormous headphones she uses to shut everyone out.

He strides towards her anyway, and mouths the only word he knows will make her let him in: 'Smoke?'

She stands up and wordlessly follows him to the balcony. It's a familiar, but odd set-up – five-minute stretches of the day spent standing next to each other, smoking cigarettes in silence. The silence is of her choosing. He often tries to punctuate it with small talk.

'It's your kryptonite, isn't it? Smoking?' he says, while flashing the boyish, crooked grin that's worked for him many, many times before, but never with Pia for some reason.

'And yours is … anything with a set of boobs and an ass?' she says snarkily. Though she's careful not to meet his gaze, her lips are curling into a quarter-smile.

If this were a romantic comedy, their meet-cute would have been two months ago, when he ran into a sobbing Pia on this very balcony during one of his smoke breaks. Back when he was new in office and she was, in her own words to him, 'not interested in socializing'. That is why she wore unusually large headphones and ate her lunches alone at her desk.

He didn't even notice her crying all the while he was unwrapping his new cigarette pack, patiently breaking off the golden foil, turning his lucky cigarette upside down and fishing out one from the back row. It was only after he lit it, took his first puff and exhaled that he noticed her shaking shoulders and faint sniffles.

His first instinct – for some bizarre reason – was to 'stub and run'. And he was about to do that when she turned around and he was momentarily arrested by those beguiling panda eyes, which were reflecting an expression that was a mix of surprise, embarrassment and sadness.

His second instinct – for some even more bizarre reason – was to offer her his cigarette.

It was like handing a pacifier to a baby. Her shoulders stopped shaking by the second drag and the tears had dried up by the fifth or the sixth. After that, she tried to apologetically return the cigarette, with the same smile. Maybe it was because he'd just been staring at her like an idiot the whole time.

He shook his head and pulled out a fresh one for himself.

'Would you like to talk about it?' he asked.

She shook her head.

'Boyfriend troubles?' he prodded again.

'Fiancé,' she said, stubbing the cigarette and going back inside.

Okay, so it wasn't the cutest meet. He got practically friend – nah – *stranger-zoned* in their very first conversation. He is glad she's actually smiling and speaking to him in multisyllables for the first time today.

'Boobs and what now?' he says, feigning shock and horror like a Victorian lady, making her smile a little wider. 'So, tell me, how does all the office gossip penetrate those jumbo headphones of yours?' He leans in closer, teasingly.

'They shield my ears, but sadly, not my eyes,' she says, with a mock sigh of disappointment.

'Is this about what happened in the unisex bathroom on the third floor?' he asks, nodding knowingly.

She half-smiles during her reply, 'Indeed.'

'It's not what it looked like,' he fakes guilt.

She raises an eyebrow at him.

'Okay, it's exactly what it looked like,' he grins, as she smiles while shaking her head in disdain. He wonders if he can make her laugh next – 'Though, in my defence, *she* started it.'

Still shaking her head, Pia stubs her cigarette and heads back inside, leaving Kabir content with his newfound knowledge of her laughter – pleasantly tinkly and infectious.

Pia

She had felt uncharacteristically confident tonight. That's why she dug out a green shift dress from the back of her closet, where it had been banished months ago for not fitting. She'd spent an hour laboriously combing out the tangles in her hair, smoothing out and teasing each curl with conditioner, serum and hair spray. She'd spent another hour watching an Instagram tutorial on contouring, the streaks of dark and pale foundation making her look like a soldier in battle trenches. She'd been generous with the eyeliner, coating her upper lids with it before letting it wander further into cat-eye territory, then following up with a thick layer of mascara and a coat of deep, dark red lipstick. Her cosmetic armour was complete, and for a while it worked. She'd felt bullet-proof.

As she'd sat on the top of the bed, to adjust the straps of her metal-studded heels, Raghav had walked in, assaulting her senses with Davidoff Blue Water. He'd looked at her and smiled, as if to say, *The old Pia is back.*

But as they enter the elevator of a high-rise building in Gurugram, on their way up to Raghav's client's apartment, Pia feels it all start to fall apart. She absentmindedly glances at Raghav's reflection in the copper-tinted mirror beside the floor panels. He towers several inches above her at six feet-something, and with each strand of hair gelled to crisp, a stubble that looks professionally groomed, and a well-tailored suit designed to hug each muscle that he spends hours honing at the gym, he looks like he's walked straight out of a scientist's laboratory – a machine designed to aesthetically please.

And standing next to him, holding his hand is … a clown. Pia notices with increasing horror that her makeup is, well, garish. Her foundation is cakey and unblended, her rouge too pink, her lipstick too red. Why, she looks five seconds away from inviting some poor child into a gutter and drowning him to his death!

Meanwhile, her hair has gone back to its original state – her curls expanding riotously, growing, seeking further territory to conquer, with zero sense of direction. And that green dress … She realizes she should have burned it when she had the chance. It's like the fabric is designed to cling to every flaw, and then hold each tyre, curve, dimple or bump up to the light. It is also painfully short – leaving her plump arms and legs outrageously bare.

'I can't go in like this …' she says to Raghav, trying to smooth her hair desperately, and somehow mentally will away some of her fat.

'What are you talking about? You look fantastic!' Raghav replies, but he isn't looking at her. She can see him arranging his pretty features into a dopey pout in the mirror. It's the same way he pouts in his gym selfies, and Pia hates it.

Before she can reply, the lift doors clang open, ushering them into a spacious apartment.

She sucks in a deep breath.

People are everywhere. Draped over white leather couches, leaning against stark, white walls that split into the hallways leading into (*six … seven?*) bedrooms.

She feels like a strange, bloated creature surrounded by impossibly gorgeous women in barely-there dresses and men in collared shirts and khakis, who give her the once-over and scoff, as she walks across the white-marbled floor, and past white tables covered in delicate, white ceramics.

The party flows, swells and rages on around her as if she was never there to begin with. People laugh, spill drinks, smoke joints, and yell over each other and the music. Unaware of her self-loathing, meaningless existence.

They finally spot their host Karan, who is just finishing up a tour of his pad with some guests.

'Hey buddy!' he says to Raghav. Although as tall as her boyfriend, Karan's on the portlier side. His handlebar moustache, maroon shirt tucked awkwardly into black trousers and potbelly blurring out the beltline lend him the aura of a hipster Air India Maharaja. This is a party to celebrate the opening of his sixth restaurant that is only a few kilometres away. Housed inside a Louvre-inspired glass pyramid – that Pia suspects is his phallic ode to himself – it's a microbrewery-cum-greenhouse.

'This guy!' Karan exclaims, introducing her boyfriend to the group he's standing with. 'He's an entrepreneur to watch out for. So, basically … you know what, you tell them, Raghav.'

Karan has the booming voice of a movie trailer narrator, and he's ensured that this audience of five is kept in suspense about Raghav's career. They stare at the latter in rapt attention.

'I source exotic ingredients for high-end restaurants like Karan's,' Raghav says, swirling his whisky around in the crystal cut glass like a connoisseur for added effect. 'Cured meats from Germany and Japan, the best truffle from Italy, fresh, leafy greens – from bok choy to Thai basil – you name it …'

'That's insane, man,' says a man wearing thick glasses, a chequered blue shirt and pastel blue pants with suspenders, i.e., Raghav's target demographic. 'I know someone else, in fact, who would be really interested in meeting you. He's starting something new in Hauz Khas …'

Raghav abandons Pia to network, and she watches him manoeuvre through the pad with the ease of a rockstar diving into the crowd from the stage, allowing them to slowly bodysurf him from one end of the room to the other.

Pia walks to the opposite side of the room, hoping to find a quiet corner where she can sit and scroll past all her social media feeds until the end of the party.

She's only halfway there when a cloud of Yves Saint Laurent's Opium descends upon her, momentarily hypnotizing her with the fragrance and the jingle of rings and bracelets that follows.

'Well, well, if it isn't little Pia – oh, you've grown a little bigger now, haven't you?' Clara, an architect who has worked on several projects alongside Raghav, including this one, eyes Pia's newly attained girth, with her glittering kohled eyes.

'Are you looking for your boyfriend? He must be around, hobnobbing with "potential clients". You know how these parties are,' Clara says in her baritonal, smoker's voice. Her tone is both conspiratorial and friendly, as though they've met more than twice. 'Come, let's go for a smoke outside,' she says, grabbing Pia's hand and leading her to the terrace before she can even reply.

Clara scares Pia, but not as much as she scares Raghav and the other guys he works with, who aren't used to competing with or desiring women like her. She has the body of a Victoria's Secret Angel and the confidence of an average Delhi guy, and the combination is disconcerting. In fact, as she leads Pia up the stairs, her first instinct is to yell '*help!*'.

Yet, she has no choice but to follow her chocolate-skinned, wavy-haired, black sari-clad predator.

'Wow,' says Pia, as she stumbles on to the sprawling, practically deserted terrace. Her eyes travel past the mini-garden and jacuzzi, to the pretty little gazebo with a Hawaiian-style bar housed in it. But that's one half of it. An iron hedge lined with creepers separates the other side that's draped in darkness.

'Penthouse privileges, baby,' Clara says, letting out a big 'whoop!'. 'He says he dropped fifteen crores on this apartment, and I believe it. The amount means nothing to him, you know. It's like a drop of water in his ocean-like *jaydaad*. God, do you think I should seduce him tonight?'

Clara enjoys shocking her audience with scandalous one-liners. Pia thinks it's her way of claiming those 'she slept her way to the top' rumours that inevitably follow powerful women everywhere. Clara had once told her the rumours did not bother her, and oddly, Pia believes her. If anything, she thinks they tickle Clara, who relishes the prospect of the poor little rich boys getting worked up over the fact that *she* got everything 'so easy'.

Pia suspects that the hideous Louvre triangle was also Clara's idea of a joke.

In fact, she feels a strange kinship with Clara in this moment. She doesn't fit in either. Instead, she stands out brilliantly. A black sari sparkling amid the sea of LBDs.

Clara lights a cigarette before handing the lighter to Pia, who fumbles with her clutch to fish out her own cigarette.

'Nevermind, take one of mine,' Clara says, her smooth

movements a jarring contrast to Pia's. 'Besides, you don't have to worry about any shit either, do you? With Raghav being the heir to his family's leather empire – in addition to whatever side business he's up to right now. And, from what I have heard, your family's just as loaded.'

Pia knows Clara comes from 'nothing' – or perhaps, that's what you would call someone from a middle-class family in West Delhi, 'who studied architecture at Magannath University, of all places', in these circles.

'We're okay,' Pia shrugs, uncomfortable at the hint of jealousy in Clara's voice. For a second, she wonders what Clara must think of someone like her – coasting on papa's money and whiling away her days at some lifestyle website until she marries a sugar daddy. The sheer laziness. The waste of privilege and potential …

She realizes she *does* care what Clara thinks of her.

'He's a hottie, too,' Clara continues, sighing dramatically, before adding, 'I heard you guys were getting hitched soon?'

'Well, nothing's fixed yet …' Pia begins, trying not to sound too cut-up about it. She so desperately doesn't want to be cast as the dried-up hag chasing after her boyfriend for a ring.

'Well, I'd say hold on to him tight until then.'

Pia has no idea where this is going, and she suspects Clara never chit-chats without it all leading to something.

Clara laughs as Pia looks at her thoughtfully. 'I'm not talking about myself. Oh, no, lord. Don't get me wrong, darling, but I'm not sure Raghav could handle me.'

Pia smiles, not the least bit offended. Instead, she replies, 'Yeah, you're right, he probably couldn't.'

'It's just that I've seen other bitches. You know … sniffing around.'

As if on cue, they hear laughter.

Pia feels a vestigial, animal-like intuition churn her belly in warning, and her body responds to it in the same brutish way. Her shoulders hunch and pupils dilate, as she cocks her head ever-so-slightly towards the direction it's coming from.

The iron hedge dividing the terrace collapses, and she feels the corners of her lips lift into a strange smile as she watches a sheepish couple emerge from behind it, scurrying towards the exit.

Pia's hand isn't her own anymore. Its fingers are splayed out awkwardly, as they twist and twirl the cigarette between them at a dangerous speed. But she is much more occupied by Raghav's hand, that's protectively clutching some girl. He doesn't look around before returning to the party.

'Pia, you're hurting yourself,' she hears Clara's voice say from far away. She looks down and sees the blazing butt of the cigarette singing the spot between her middle and ring finger. There's an angry red scar forming there, and the smell of burnt skin wafts in the air, but she can't feel anything.

Jerking her head to Clara, she brings the cigarette to her lips and sucks on it till her cheeks are hollowed out and her lungs choked up, not stopping till the glowing ember tip is touching the edge of her lips.

'Pia, no!' Clara yells, sounding terrified, before gasping, 'Your eyes…'

Finally, as though a spell has been broken, Pia exhales. Doubling over, she continues to cough and wheeze as a whole cigarette's worth of smoke slowly exits her body and envelops the two women in a hazy, cancerous cloud. Clara's bangles jingle loudly while she pats Pia on the back, the latter trying desperately to gulp in the fresh air. 'What happened to my eyes?' Pia rasps.

'For a moment, they were yellow? But maybe it was a reflection of all the fairy lights or something,' Clara shakes her head. 'How could you finish an entire cigarette, filter and all, in one breath? That was pure Rajinikanth-level insanity.'

'I don't know what happened,' Pia says, as she feels it all hit her together – the burn in her chest, the dull ache in her heart and the unpleasant, jerky sensation in her stomach, as though the very centre of her gravity has shifted.

Oh, you know exactly what happened, she hears a familiar voice respond. But it isn't Clara's. It is coming from Pia's belly, that's churning still, as an ancient monster unfurls itself in her core. It expands and contracts, while gasping for its first breath in years.

Its scales bristle her insides, as it whispers – *Now what, Pia?*

Pia tries to ignore the voice, focusing on what Clara is saying instead.

'I'm sorry, darling, I didn't want you to find out this way … I just didn't expect him to be this stupid … Start off at a party, while you're right there … God! Men are pigs,' she rambles on, adding, 'Her name is Sonia. An Instagram model. She's barely twenty … Don't worry, babe … he'll come back to you. They always do.'

But Clara's casual words are a stark contrast to her hand holding Pia's in a death grip. 'I'd suggest you still go through with that wedding. Just make sure you bleed him dry with the alimony,' she whispers.

Pia doesn't scream, when she comes back down and sees Raghav standing in the middle of the room, extolling the high quality of his exotic ingredients to a new audience. 'Yeah, like for Oktoberfest, I had supplied bratwurst from Germany to Karan …'

She doesn't claw his face when he turns to her and smiles, acting like his dick has been in his pants this whole time.

And she doesn't run away into the black night, leaving Raghav, his idiotic friends and this ugly evening behind her.

Instead, she sips on wine, as the voice in her belly asks her the same question over and over, *What now, Pia?*

When they're back in the lift, Pia gazes at Raghav's reflection in the mirror once again. He looks even more beautiful now – the shadows, the yellow lights and the copper tint acting as the perfect filter. His face, even when tired, is Adonis-like, Pia realizes.

You're settling for him, she recalls Ila's imaginary words from this morning. They sound hilarious now, out here in the real world.

Yet, she has to admit that he doesn't make her heart jump or ache in the same way anymore.

In fact, she isn't sure if he ever did.

What he *had* done was make her mother almost squeal in delight the day Pia had brought him home. He'd made her sister say 'whatta catch!' in surprise, and even her father cleared his throat in approval.

Her family had acted like she'd won the lottery, barely hiding their surprise over how Pia had managed to reel in such a catch.

The thought of going back to them and telling them she messed it all up makes her shudder violently.

She lifts her eyes towards her own reflection, expecting to see the same sad, scary clown staring back at her.

What she sees makes her gasp.

Those eyes – completely dilated, yellow and blazing with pure venom. Pia doesn't recognize them as her own. She watches the amber-eyed Pia in the mirror play with the itching and stinging cigarette wound between her fingers, just the way she is doing right now. The reflection continues to copy her movements closely, tauntingly, holding her gaze … until, suddenly, its eyes turn to Raghav, who is looking down at his phone, scrolling past memes. Pia holds her breath, as she continues to stare at her doppelgänger, only letting it out when the doors slide open.

Just before they shut again, Pia spies a glance at the CCTV above the empty guard's desk in the foyer. Her reflection is still there in the mirror with its teeth bared in an unnatural, horrifying grin. It lifts its fingers up slightly, before curling them back in slowly, as though waving Pia goodbye.

'Why don't you spend the night tonight?' Pia asks Raghav in the car, on their way back home.

She had meant to make it sound casual, but it feels illicit – like some kind of an indecent proposal. Maybe because they haven't had sex in months.

'I actually have an … early morning meeting,' he replies, brushing his hand lightly against hers folded tightly in her lap. 'I'll pick you up at noon for the mehendi.'

She flinches slightly. Getting out of the car wordlessly, she slams the door behind her.

Five seconds later, he's gone.

He'll come back to you. They always do, she remembers Clara saying.

And Pia knows that when he does, she'll make him pay.

Oh, she would bleed him dry.

She doesn't sleep the whole night.

Instead, the first thing she does is to find Sonia's Instagram feed.

Sonia Sharma. 20.

Eternal dreamer. Hippie Child. Yoga chick. Vegan.

'Wow, Raghav, *so* original,' she scoffs out loud, lighting up a cigarette.

Still in her green dress and heels, Pia throws herself onto her bed and scrolls past pictures of Sonia twisted and contorted into a series of impossible-looking *asanas*, while dressed in skimpy sports bras and shorts. Her feed is also peppered with giant buddha-bowls filled with avocados, hummus, cherry tomatoes, brown rice and tofu. Every once in a while, she soul-searches in the mountains, and more often than not, she unwinds in a bikini at the beach. There are several pictures of quotes with the mountains or seas in the backdrop, each extolling the strength of women by comparing them to wolves and flowers.

Pia scrolls past her whole feed thrice, smoking furiously, letting the cigarette ash spill onto her bed.

At 4 a.m., she wanders to the kitchen. She bends over and unclasps the straps of her heels, before throwing them over to the side and opening the fridge.

She gazes at the contents and does the Keto math – dividing and subtracting each item's protein, carb and fat content, trying to somehow fit it into her daily intake. She almost compromises with a bacon omelette before muttering, 'Fuck it.'

Barely a few seconds later, all the food inside is scattered on the floor. She starts with the loaf of bread – the tasteless, soggy carbs soothing her soul – before devouring a chocolate cake with both hands.

I am a monster, she tells herself, while stuffing her face until her jaws and stomach hurt.

Once she's done, she goes upstairs to the bathroom. Ritualistically extracting her weighing machine from the cupboard underneath the sink, she takes off each article of her clothing before stepping onto it. She looks past the unsightly rolls of her stomach to the number the machine reflects.

She has gained ten kilos in the last six months, just in time for her sister's mehendi. She looks at the lehenga hanging behind the door – the one that stopped fitting her months ago – with belly-churning panic and turns towards the toilet.

Lifting up the lid, she sticks a finger into her throat and hurls into it loudly and violently.

When Pia finally slips back into bed, she falls asleep, dreaming of Sonia's perfect, twig-like body.

3

FIVE DAYS TO THE WEDDING

Pia

'It's your sister's wedding in four days, how does that make you feel?' her psychiatrist of more than a decade, Dr Agarwal – a bald, jowly, total Sarkari-type middle-aged man – asks her. He drums his pen against his prescription pad impatiently, itching to write Pia a long-ass list of medication, she's sure. His office is anything but the calm space she has seen in American sitcoms, where psychiatrists sit in plush chairs and speak in hushed notes to patients lying on cushy couches.

No, Dr Agarwal's aesthetic is more regular: a wooden, glass-topped table, covered in depressing, obsolete knick-knacks from the sixties, like paperweights, pencil sharpeners, a globe, and ceramic souvenirs, while Pia sits on the wooden chair opposite it, the scratchy straw of the seat making her bum itch. The unforgiving backrest forces her spine to a ninety-degree angle. The lighting is harsh too, like a police interrogation chamber. It's no wonder patients end up sharing their most intimate secrets with him.

'I don't know? Happy, I guess? Mostly indifferent. Khushi and I—' Pia clears her throat – clarifying for what feels like the zillionth time – 'We aren't very close.'

Seriously, does he even know her? *What does he even write in that pad anyway?* Though she knows his 'official' diagnosis of her, Pia doubts that's the entire truth. It feels more like a label her mother wanted slapped on to her hurriedly fifteen years ago.

'It must be complicated. Seeing your younger sister get married before you,' he continues to ply her with his inane observations.

Pia glares at him. She hates this man, but he is the only one her mother trusts with her, well, *history*. The problem with this whole setup, though, is that it feels a lot like sharing her most intimate thoughts with an uncle*ji*. Either way, he makes up for his lack of empathy and subtlety with those prescription-writing skills. Pia's sure, every time he looks at her, all he sees is a lab rat to try his drugs on.

She continues glaring at him, refusing to dignify his last statement with a response.

'You've gained more weight since the last time we met. Still having problems with emotional eating?' he asks her.

Pia suppresses the urge to say, *Well, you're no underwear model yourself, doc,* seeing as how his own potbelly seems to be fighting to break free from his piss-yellow shirt right now.

'I think it's the pills you gave me,' she replies pointedly instead. 'Perhaps, if we could look at a lower dosage …'

He moves on quickly to – 'How are things with your partner?'

She hasn't had a decent conversation or sex with her boyfriend in the last six months, and he's fucking a twenty-year-old social-media influencer, but obviously she can't tell *uncle* that.

'I don't know. Fine, I guess? Again, the pills make it hard though, to be, you know, present. He complains about me being zoned out a lot,' Pia says.

'I would advise against lower dosage,' he replies, his pen and pad already poised to make his point.

'Fine,' she snaps. 'No, then nothing else. Everything's great.'

'What about social life?'

'Non-existent,' she shrugs, 'Just the way I like it …'

The pen goes scribble-scribble at that. Then he looks up again, and asks, 'Has the voice returned?'

Pia groans loudly and throws her head back, her fists balled up against her brow. 'No. How many times will we go through this? It happened fourteen years ago. Don't you think it's past time we moved on?'

'We are quite short-tempered today, aren't we?' he asks, adding suspiciously, 'You *are* taking your medication?'

'Of course,' she says, suddenly growing nervous. He scribbles furiously in his cursed pad, making her feel foolish for her outburst and terrified of the repercussions.

Dr Agarwal also happens to be a snitch – none of that doctor-patient confidentiality stuff for him.

'It's just … I should be getting to work soon,' she says meekly, her balled-up fists back by her sides, her back ramrod straight, her demeanour that of a puppy who has just been reprimanded.

He hands her a piece of paper with the same long list of medications. She knows every inscrutable scrawl on it by heart.

Just like she knows he will call her mom up in the evening to give her the play-by-play of this session.

Neeta

'Holy crap! Looks like someone puked marigolds all over the place!' she cringes at the crass words, which are tinged with that familiar I-went-and-studied-in-America-for-a-year accent. She realizes once again that she can't stand her daughter's boyfriend, Raghav, despite the fact he is all her matrimonial column dreams come true – six feet tall, fair, handsome, with family business, six-figure salary and from the Khatri caste, along with having studied in America for a year.

'Don't worry about it, ma … No one's ever gonna be good enough for your precious Pia anyway,' Khushi, her younger daughter, had scoffed two years back. (Khushi had been convinced since the age of eight that Neeta clearly loved her older daughter more and had alternated between scoffing at Neeta and switching to a pitiful Dickensian orphan narrative as a result.)

Okay, Raghav may not be entirely *wrong*, Neeta thinks, as she heads out to the main entrance of the bungalow to admire her and her right-hand man Raju's handiwork.

It does look like someone vomited endless strings of marigolds and fairy lights over the recently renovated Bhandari ancestral house in Sainik Farms. They snake the imposing entrance gates of the farmhouse in some nonsensical, criss-cross pattern, and then circle each of the bushes lining the driveway right up to the bungalow, which is practically smothered in the same, giving it the appearance of being hurled on indefinitely by that possessed girl from *The Exorcist*.

But isn't that the whole point of a Punjabi wedding?

Neeta closes her eyes, taking in the overwhelming, now borderline intrusive, fragrance of the marigold, and imagines the Bhandari bungalow coming alive five days from now under the flowers and twinkling lights. Neeta can almost hear the faint *dhol* beats of the *baraat* marching to the gates. It's so close she can hear her judgemental chachu from Jalandhar marvelling at how 'no expense was spared' when the bartender pours Chivas Regal into his glass.

And he'd be correct. A smug smile creeps across her face as her daughter appears in her dream sequence, in a no-expense-spared, Sabyasachi-designed wedding lehenga. She would spare no money or marigolds to show how much she loves her beautiful daughter. *(And who knows? Maybe that would put an end to Khushi's 'may I please have some more gruel' act?*)

The intensity of her vision combines with her self-righteous anger over Raghav's off-hand comment, just as

Raju walks by in a sweat-stained baniyan, his dark, skinny arms filled with another batch of marigolds. 'Throw some of that into the swimming pool also,' she orders, deciding she won't be dictated how much marigold is too much by a man who refuses to propose to her daughter. He meets all of the matrimonial prerequisites except one – *a desire to marry*.

'Is that a new BMW standing at the back?' Raghav is speaking in the same obnoxious accent. 'N-a-iiiice.'

Pia is trailing behind him, dressed in some dull, vomit-green salwar-kameez-type outfit that Neeta's certain she fished out of her cupboard five minutes before leaving.

'Dad says it's not really *dahej* if I am the one driving it,' Khushi scoffs again as she envelops both him and Pia in a hug.

'Shut up, Khushi. It's not dahej because your fiancé can afford a dozen BMWs,' Neeta shushes her, not just because it's a fact, but also to nip any of Raghav's dreams of being gifted a BMW in the bud. He laughs, before wandering off to search for the bar.

'Why aren't you wearing the lehenga?' she asks Pia, who responds with a shrug.

'Yeah, or you could have just turned up in your night suit!' Khushi pipes in.

Neeta glares at her.

'What? She could have made more of an effort for her sister's wedding. Brushed her hair, perhaps?'

'Stop it, Khushi,' Neeta says in that same tone she used to shut them up as toddlers. It still works.

However, she can't deny that Pia *does* look awful. She

appears to have not slept, taken her meds, or brushed her hair – in days.

She resists the urge to drag her into the bedroom to rinse and scrub her clean and untangle every knot in her hair. To shake her by the shoulders and tell her to get it together before the guests arrived.

Why does Pia always create new reasons for their relatives to bitch more about her?

Neeta would never play favourites between her two daughters. She just loves them both differently. And contrary to Khushi's belief, Pia had been more difficult to love – from the days she began growing in Neeta's womb.

It started with the most intense morning sickness, which made her want to claw and rip the baby out of her uterus.

Even when things settled down, baby Pia had a penchant for trouble. At some point, she almost strangled herself with her own umbilical cord. She'd shift, turn, and kick constantly, until she lodged herself somewhere dangerously low in Neeta's belly around the second or third trimester. Neeta was placed on bedrest for the rest of her lonesome, anxious pregnancy, feeling resentment, guilt, motherly love and the baby – all growing in her belly at the same time.

Neeta was so glad when her daughter was finally out. She could now reclaim her own body while also protecting her baby, unlike when she was wandering around her uterus uncontrollably and unchecked.

Pia was right here in front of her, she'd thought as she held her newborn daughter in her arms at the hospital, within sight and reach. What kind of trouble could she get herself into this way?

Neeta almost laughs at the naivety of that last statement.

From the kitchen window, she watches Pia helplessly wander around in the courtyard where the mehendi ceremony is more than halfway through now.

'She's a carbon copy of you,' Neeta's friends and relatives had exclaimed when they first saw her miniature version swaddled in a thick blanket, even though her skin was still a wrinkly red and her features barely formed squiggles. Neeta couldn't see it until the day she saw it all too clearly – the same large, bewildered eyes, wide, unsure smile and long, loopy nose, and a face that mimicked Neeta's expressions and behavioural ticks to the T. As a result, Neeta can read her daughter all too easily.

Right now, she looks like Bambi after the hunter shot his mother – nervous, clumsy and on thin ice.

Khushi's holding court a few feet away, while sitting in the grass, with the *mehendiwala* henna-ing her hand from fingertips to elbows. She is sipping beer through a straw and chatting with other tipsy chachis-mamis. Between big gulps, she shouts out at the top of her lungs the lyrics to the Bollywood song currently playing, as her college friends dance on a makeshift dance floor in the garden. She has her mother's smile too, but that's about it. The rest of her is delicate and yet perfectly moulded features and limbs, all too sharp to be vulnerable. Her yellow lehenga reveals her perfectly toned midriff, while her straight, black hair with golden highlights is parted to one side, a sparkling jhoomar hanging off the other.

The Barbie to Pia's Bambi.

Neeta feels an umbilical tug towards her Bambi, but she can hear Khushi and her husband's voices in her head, like a Greek improvised chorus:

Let her be.
You coddle her too much.
How will she learn if you don't let her go ...

Neeta notices Raghav animatedly talking to her husband, Ajit, who has been as dismissive as Khushi about Neeta's dislike for their potential son-in-law.

Unlike Neeta, Ajit doesn't even bother to act like one of his daughters isn't his favourite. He has always seemed a little afraid of Pia's checked-out, quiet demeanour. Twenty-seven years ago, he had been surprised to meet a silent, sage-like baby, wondering aloud if all the Pampers commercials with happy, bouncy toddlers had all just been a big lie. So disappointed was he that he would switch to his Supreme Court lawyer-speak, directing his impotent rage at the television, while mumbling something about 'gross misrepresentation of babies' under his breath. Despite this, he would spend hours trying to make her smile – mimicking different voices and bringing in toys that quacked, mooed and barked – only to be met with colicky howls.

Then, when Khushi giggled, drooled and waddled into that same nursery two years later, he couldn't help but be charmed by this baby, who was equally enamoured with his quacks, moos and barks. He spent all of his spare time moulding his younger daughter into his image and was endlessly amused when toddler Khushi would don his oversized robes and preside over their dining table, crying 'order, order' and bringing down the rolled-up newspaper gavel next to her lunch, spilling *raita* everywhere.

Meanwhile, his elder child drifted further away, becoming a mystery that he could never quite solve.

Still, Neeta remembers how happy they *both* were the first day Pia brought Raghav home. They'd been hunting for a groom for her since three years before that, only to be met with her blank stares and deathly silence. They had even held up Khushi's *roka* to her high-school boyfriend, Kaushal, for a year or two, before giving up and settling on dates. Then, suddenly, Raghav had materialized from thin air. He was so great on paper, and visibly smitten by her daughter, that Neeta had mentally promised the gods a trip to Vaishno Devi that very summer as a thank-you.

'Pia looked happy, didn't she?' Ajit whispered to Neeta contentedly that night in bed. 'Who knew our daughter could actually *smile*?'

Returning to present day, Neeta glances out the window again, where Pia's still lost … and a little drunk. *Now it's getting too painful.* She asks one of the maids to fetch her in.

'Are you supposed to be mixing your medication with alcohol like that?' She points to the glass of white wine in her daughter's hand the minute she walks in, looking visibly relieved. Neeta passes over a cucumber and a chopping board to her.

Pia shrugs, taking another sip before grabbing the cucumber and looking at it in a disoriented manner.

'I've been calling you for the last two days. Why didn't you pick up? Also, what on earth is this salwar kameez!' Neeta continues reprimanding her, as she takes the cucumber back from Pia and starts working on it herself, chopping off a bit of the front and rubbing the two uneven halves to get rid of the bitterness.

'You don't like it? It's yours,' Pia slouches against the counter, watching her mother work.

Neeta studies the outfit, with its poofy sleeves and strange bib-like design of orange spirals on the front. 'Oh yes, it is,' Neeta remembers, then mutters, 'Why you would wear an 80s' suit to your sister's wedding is beyond me.' And before she can help it, 'Also, it *barely* fits you.'

'I am just worried, beta,' she tries to do some damage-control the minute the words leave her mouth. She lifts her daughter's chin, and looks straight into her eyes, the same chocolate-brown as her own but blank. Neeta can't read a thing.

Pia had learnt early on that if she kept her expressions entirely and deathly still, Neeta couldn't use her mom superpowers on her anymore.

The poker face has always annoyed Neeta to no end, and right now, she couldn't stop the words exiting her mouth, 'You need to take care of your health. It's been what … ten kilos, in the last eight months?'

The silence that follows is deafening. Pia's expressionless still.

'*Yahan mera tumhaare saath* keto *kar kar ke* five kilos lose *ho gaya*, and you've just been piling it on. Are you following the diet at all?'

For a moment, she can read her daughter again: *Annoyance.*

'Dr Agarwal *said* the medication would get in the way …' Pia begins, but Neeta interrupts her.

'He also said that you could control the effects with diet and exercise, beta. Anyway, have you and Raghav discussed marriage again?'

Pia sighs, which is the only encouragement Neeta needs to continue.

'I just don't understand why it's taking him so long. You've been together for two years now. How much more will you do this "getting to know each other" drama. His business seems to be taking off as well.'

'I don't know,' her daughter says coldly, looking away, absentmindedly twiddling the stem of her wine glass.

'What you don't know is men. First of all, he's younger than you. On top of it, they don't have to worry about getting married on time like women do. And if he's enjoying this live-in and all, why would he commit?'

'Please stop it, mom …'

She looks at Pia sternly, as she says, 'I've seen his wandering eye. My mother's intuition tells me you need to lock it down soon.'

Fear.

'Also you really should lose some weight.'

'Ma!'

'What? Men are visual creatures. I still put on lipstick and blow-dry my hair for your father after thirty-five years.'

Pia's mask thaws completely as she dumps her now-empty wine glass a little too violently into the kitchen sink, before heading towards the door.

'What did I say wrong?' Neeta is exasperated – with herself for saying these things and her daughter, for leaving her with no choice but to say them.

'You're really callous sometimes,' Pia screams tearily, before she is out the door.

'Because I am your mother. Because I worry!' she yells to her daughter's back.

Pia would never know just how much Neeta worried.

For the self-destructive foetus Pia.

For the colicky baby Pia.

For the friendless and bullied teen Pia.

And even more so, after what happened ...

When, for the first time since she gave birth to Pia, Neeta had wished she could have her daughter crawl back inside her womb instead, not sure whether it was to save her baby from the world or the other way round.

When Pia leaves, Neeta sighs and gazes out of the kitchen window, taking in all the *shor* of the shaadi outside.

Instead of letting it haunt her, Neeta now tries to think of the day – when she walked into thirteen-year-old Pia's bedroom and saw what she did – as a wake-up call.

4

FOUR DAYS TO THE WEDDING

Kabir

Pia is standing in the parking lot, fiddling with her phone and shifting her weight impatiently from the balls of her feet to her toes. Her large, bright blue bag is slung over her shoulders. It keeps slipping off, and she adjusts the strap until she gets tired and dumps it angrily on to the floor, where she sits on it.

That is when he chooses to exit the wings and play knight in shining armour, asking, 'Do you need a ride home?'

As she smiles at him, she lifts her head, squinting her eyes and raising a hand to shield them from the sun. 'No, thank you.'

'Ah. Waiting for your fiancé?' he asks, crouching beside her.

She holds up her bare ring finger at him. 'Not my fiancé.'

'That's what you told me …' he begins, before he

puts two and two together, 'to get rid of me, of course.'

Her grin grows wider.

'So … boyfriend, then?' he says, offering her a cigarette, which she refuses with a shake of her head. He lights one up for himself.

'Yup.'

'Let me guess,' he says, exhaling the smoke dramatically. 'He has a big, shiny car.'

A flashy, red Jaguar rolls into the parking lot just as Pia grabs his cigarette. 'Shit,' she says softly, and stubs it reflexively, instead of handing it back to him.

'That's my ride,' she says, with an apologetic smile.

'And that's mine,' Kabir says, pressing the button on his car key remote.

A beat-up white Alto lets out a sad beep from the corner of the first row, as his smile mirrors hers.

5

TWO DAYS TO THE WEDDING

Pia

Pia's heart sinks as she tries on the blouse for her sister's wedding. A victim of her mother's hubris (she'd told the tailor to make all clothes at least one size smaller, since she was convinced she would whip Pia into shape by then), Pia now calls out to her from inside in a humiliated voice – 'It doesn't fit.'

'*What do you mean it doesn't fit?*' her mother's thunderous voice is embarrassingly loud and audible to not just the tailor, but all the other customers crammed into the tiny basement shop, located somewhere in the bowels of GK-1 M-block market.

Pia stops trying to not breathe in an effort to make herself shrink one size smaller, and then almost rips off the stringy, golden number.

'It's too tight,' she reiterates tearily to her, as she storms out of the changing room and dumps the bedazzled piece of cloth into her mother's hand.

'Masterji,' her mother pleads to the tailor, and he nods at her, before he tells her he'll take care of it.

'*Do din mein shaadi hai,*' her mother cribs on the way to the car, 'And now we will have to get the blouse fixed at the last minute. I just hope he does it correctly. Also, weren't you thirty-two inches the last time, *ab yeh* thirty-four *kaise ho gaya?*'

'I was thirty-three,' Pia defends herself bitterly, but she knows it's of no use. It's begun.

'It's just that … we got you yoga classes and a nutritionist. What else can *we* do? It's you who needs to put in the effort in the end.

'Are you sleeping properly? You don't look like you're sleeping. Your under-eye circles are getting darker. I am booking an appointment with Yasmine. We need to figure out what to do with those … and your hair,' her mother reaches out and runs a hand through her rough, tangled mane.

Pia looks out of the window, zoning out from the rest of her mother's diatribe.

Every time she is with her mom, Pia turns thirteen again.

Since that day, even as her limbs stretched and grew and her body began to morph into a woman's, her brain froze and she was cryogenically preserved as that monster.

At twenty-seven, she still navigates life with the help of an elaborate system of rules and rituals that her mother set in place fourteen years ago.

For these past fourteen years, Pia has watched her mother vet her friends, screen her phone bills and check her eyes every single day to see if they are the right amount of hazy.

From a bedroom in the remotest corner of their bungalow, Pia has now upgraded to a flat that her parents bought her. It's an hour away from work, but half an hour away from theirs.

Every morning, she joins her mother at yoga, and every night ends in a phone call detailing the day's events.

'You *need structure*,' her mother reminds her every day, as she helps Pia stock up the fridge, and sort her laundry and bills.

'You *need friends*,' her mom says casually, every evening, when she inevitably lands up again for chai and Kurkure.

It's right there. So clear, as though in writing. Unspoken yet verbalized every moment of every day -

'You need *me*.'

6

ONE DAY BEFORE THE WEDDING

Pia

She wiggles uncomfortably up to the garden of the five-star hotel that has been turned into a Moroccan harem or Lucknawi brothel – it is unclear what the theme for the cocktail is.

Pia feels like a mermaid in the royal blue, shiny fishtail gown that's practically moulded to her body. It makes the simple feat of walking impossible, so she has to flop around like a fish out of water, which is actually a fitting metaphor for tonight.

A hot-pink-and-royal-purple-coloured tent has been set up on the grounds. Luxury cabanas line the swimming pool, while shirtless, six-packed, harem pants-clad waiters approach the guests with platters of kebabs and hummus. A few feet away, there are dozens of tables decorated with hookahs and heavy lanterns with scented tea lights burning inside. In the centre of it all is a massive *Mughal-E-Azam*-inspired stage – covered in a Persian rug, with white *gaddas* on each side and long white columns erected at each of the four ends – lit up in bright blue. A group of classical Indian musicians occupy one mattress, playing the instrumental version of 'Pyaar Kiya toh Darna Kya'.

Pia thinks it is rather bold of her family to draw inspiration from Bollywood's most tragic love story.

'Aunty?' she hears a voice behind her and turns around to see Raghav standing there, dressed in a custom black and gold sherwani, holding a kebab skewer in one hand and a glass of whisky in the other.

'Fuck. Pia?' he says, after doing a double-take. 'Wow, you look incredible, babe!'

'Nice save, but you literally just called me aunty,' she sneers.

'Yeah, because I thought you were your mom, who is smokin',' he says solemnly.

'That's just disturbing, Raghav,' she snaps, grabbing one of his kebabs and resentfully popping it into her mouth.

'You've been avoiding me,' he says, offering her the rest of his skewer.

'Well, yeah, I have been busy …' she says, which isn't entirely false. The humiliation at the hands of her mother and masterji, almost made her forget about her humiliation at the hands of Raghav.

'Would you like me to get you something? More kebabs?' he offers, as if this would make up for some of the cheating.

She shakes her head.

'Can you walk in that thing?' he goes on, eyeing her with utmost pity.

'No,' Pia replies, sighing.

Thankfully, her mother appears in front of them, dressed in a sari the same colour as Pia's gown, and dripping in diamonds.

Of course, Pia sighs.

It's as if she's watching a hotter, more elegant version of herself gliding around. Pia hobbles closer to her.

'Raghav just mistook me for you. Are you happy now?' she grimaces.

'Really?' her mother laughs in response. 'I'm flattered, beta,' she says, graciously smiling at Raghav, like she's forgotten all about their bitching session in the kitchen a few days ago.

'There's no way I'm going to make it through tonight,' Pia says to her mother, as Raghav wanders off in search of more kebabs. Her mother pats her back consolingly, as they stare at the packed venue.

'Lovely it looks, *na*?' she asks Pia, beaming with pride at her handiwork. 'It's absolutely amazing,' says Pia, knowing just how hard her mother's worked.

Neeta smiles back, squeezing her hand. When she turns to face her daughter, her smile fades slightly. 'Go easy on the kebabs, beta,' she says, grabbing the skewer from Pia's hand and placing it on the plate of a passing server. 'The kale salad is to die for by the way,' she adds not-so-subtly.

'I saw you two from far away and thought, "*Arre*, who are these hot sisters?"' Bubbly bua yells from behind. She is dressed in an Abu Jani–Sandeep Khosla maroon lehenga, accessorized with a heavy, gold, medieval-torture-device-like necklace, that starts at her neck and extends all the way to her cleavage.

'And who are you – *Padmaavat ki* Deepika Padukone?' her mother replies.

They both crack up, as Bubbly bua asks, 'Now, where is the third sister?'

'She's just getting ready. Another ten to fifteen minutes.'

Then, grabbing Pia's cheeks as though she were a five-year-old, Bubbly bua screams, '*Bas! Ab agla* number is yours!'

Pia smiles in reply, which is the only encouragement she needs to break into the 'Apna Time Aayega' rap from *Gully Boy* to emphasize her point, before laughing and moving away to terrorize other relatives.

Stunned and horrified, Pia grabs a shot from the nearest shirtless server. Looking at her mother, as if this was all her fault, she swallows it in one go.

'You know what, I am going to have a shot every time someone tells me I have put on weight, or sings 'Apna Time Aayega' to me tonight!' she snaps.

'Come on, Pia. She was just joking … And you are on medication. No more shots,' her mother tells her, before getting distracted by another set of guests.

An hour later, Pia has abandoned the game herself, because she is sure she is one shot away from liver poisoning. In fact, she thinks she's hallucinating as well. She could have sworn she saw Kabir five seconds ago.

It *is* Kabir, she realizes when he materializes again – ridiculously tall, dark, lean and cute – except more traditional-looking. She squints at this maroon bandhgala-clad visage of him, standing and grinning at her, before holding up a finger tentatively and poking him with it in the chest.

'Are you checking to see if I am real?' Kabir laughs. His deep voice confirms it's him, as well as does funny things to her. She feels her heartbeat quicken, as the rest of the world fades away.

She notices that he's so tall, he always leans to one side a little, like the Tower of Pisa. His nose is a little crooked too, and his smile lopsided, with those dimples denting his cheek.

'There was a crooked man, and he walked a crooked mile …' she starts singing the nursery rhyme, before realizing she doesn't know the next line. 'Oh god, I am really wasted,' she then sighs, feeling a little wobbly.

She runs a hand through his wavy, unruly hair, deciding she loves it.

'So am I,' he replies, steadying her against him, and grabbing her hand, repositioning it by her side. 'In fact, I thought I saw two of you ten minutes back.'

'The other was my mother,' Pia says, waving her hand. 'Wait, what exactly are you even doing here?'

'My cousin is an intern here. He usually gives me and my friends a heads-up on the big, fat, juiciest weddings,' he says with a crooked grin. 'That's them out there, loading up on the kebabs,' he points to a group of over-enthusiastic bandhgala-clad men by a food counter.

'You mean, you attend these things *voluntarily*? Gross,' she fake-shudders.

'What's there to not love? Free food. Good booze. Although I do admit, this whole setup is very Karan-Johar-on-crack,' he says, appraising his surroundings. 'Speaking of which, what's with the shirtless waiters?'

'Aesthetics,' Pia replies, quite knowledgeable for someone with no knowledge about what is going on.

'So, I am guessing you are here as a legit guest then?' he asks.

She nods, before adding dramatically, 'Of all the weddings in all the towns in all the world, he walks into my sister's.'

The way he looks at her at the end of that sentence makes her breath catch in her throat.

He clears his, before saying, 'So, umm, the fiancé's here too?'

She nods, pointing to a counter close to where his friends are standing.

'Wow, he's *cute*,' Kabir says, mimicking a thirteen-year-old girl. 'Could easily be one of these shirtless waiters,' he adds a bit resentfully.

'Anyway,' Pia cuts him off. 'Let's go.'

'Where to?' he asks, placing a hand on her back, and following her as she sloppily navigates the grass and the crowd. His touch singes her, but she doesn't look behind.

'Behind the *jhaadis*,' she replies.

'Pia, I know I look pretty good in this bandhgala and it's hard to keep your hands off me and everything, but I imagined our first time together to be a little more romantic,' he says, his voice a tad bit deeper.

'I meant for a smoke, you idiot,' she says, determinedly

staring ahead, ignoring the shivers his last sentence sends down her spine.

'Right, that does make more sense,' he replies, grabbing two cocktails from the bar along the way.

She wobbles to the bush as fast as her dress will allow her. It isn't hard for him to catch up.

'Alright, the show is,' – she clicks her cellphone screen on – 'yup, it's beginning in 5, 4, 3 …'

They are safely tucked behind the bush, with cigarettes lit and drinks secured, as a tall, hefty, imposing, moustachioed man in his early sixties – dressed in a gold sherwani and matching gold turban – walks up to the stage.

'All right, ladies and gentlemen, boys and girls, settle down. Now, many of you may be wondering where the beautiful bride is …' he says into the mic.

'Oh, no,' Pia groans, even as the crowd goes wild.

'I can't decide if this guy is too old to be an emcee or too drunk,' Kabir whispers.

'That's because he's my father,' Pia whispers back through gritted teeth, watching Kabir choke on his drink in response.

'I am so sorry,' he says, but she can't tell what he's apologizing for – his previous words or her father.

'Well, then we shouldn't make you wait anymore for her, shall we?' her dad's voice booms, as louder cheers erupt in the audience. 'So, *aap sab dil thaam ke baithiye* – especially you, Kaushal,' he says, addressing the groom sitting in the front row, with a wink.

Pia groans again.

The lights dim dramatically, creating an air of anticipation. It clearly works, since Kabir is peering over curiously, as Pia rolls her eyes and sucks on the cigarette.

Khushi appears stage centre, her back to the crowd. She's dressed in a silver lehenga, and Pia's surprised her mother let her wear something *this* backless to her own cocktail, with no dupatta in sight.

She's also holding up two diyas.

'*Mera chain vain sab ujda* …' Alisha Chinai's honey-dripping voice fills the surroundings.

Khushi wiggles the dias and her bum to the music.

'*Zaalim nazar hata leeee.*'

More *thumkas*.

When she turns around during the first 'kajra re', people scream like it's a death metal concert.

The reluctant groom joins her somewhere along the third stanza. Lumbering behind her like a chimpanzee, he waves his arms and legs around in a way that implies he hates rhythm because it murdered his family and stole his childhood.

'What's a wedding without some family action?' her father says, before placing the mic carefully on the gadda, as her mother joins him on the stage, and the speakers blast the opening beats of '*Maahi Ve*'.

'Karan. Johar. On crack,' Kabir mouths the words to Pia, before she screams, 'Oh fuck, I'm next!'

Handing her drink to him, she starts hobbling to the stage, ignoring his cries of 'please hydrate before you do this'.

Though she's practised the steps to '*Lamberghini*' a

hundred times before with her sister and mother, Pia has always done so in track pants and a loose tee – and more importantly – while she was completely sober.

However, when she's finally standing on stage, Pia realizes her brain and hands are no longer in her control, while her chest and legs are straitjacketed by the gown. She hears the opening beats of the song.

All of these facts would ideally make her panic, but when she sees Kabir standing in the audience, smiling and already waving about his cellphone in the air – in tribute, she guesses – she feels calm, and a strange, unfamiliar emotion – *happiness*?

She feels that straitjacket loosen and unfurl, just like that *thing* in her belly. The thing that's now telling her –

So, what if Raghav's cheating on you … Kabir seems all too ripe for the picking, doesn't he?

She closes her eyes, nodding to the voice, hypnotized by it. Her body floats effortlessly to the music, as though it suddenly doesn't belong to her anymore. It's doing things of its own accord. Even though she knows she's no longer in control of it, she's far from panic. In fact, it feels a little too good, and a little too familiar, to give up the reins for a while.

Aww, look at him. Look at the way he looks at you. You can have him, if you want him.

In that moment, Pia truly does believe she can. She's still floating, as though hypnotized. She feels ethereal and almost Sufi, like the words and the melody are flowing through her.

When the song ends, she opens her eyes to look at

Kabir, and finds him still standing there, grinning ear-to-ear.

Once they step off the stage, Khushi snaps at her, 'What the fuck just happened? I thought we had practised this enough. I thought you could do it in your sleep, not do it while you're sleeping!'

'I don't understand ...' Pia feels confused.

'Pia, you just wandered around the stage ... lost. Are you on drugs or something?' her sister thunders.

Her mother appears behind them, seconding her sister with, 'I thought I told you to stop drinking?'

'Unbelievable,' Khushi snaps, before walking off.

'Wow, Bridezilla much?' she hears Kabir whisper in her ear, as he gently starts leading her away from the crowd.

'I am used to it,' she replies, butterflies filling her stomach as his fingers stroke her wrist reassuringly while they walk past the sea of people.

'How bad was it?' she says, slumping down on the grass when they are back at their hiding spot. Her eyes are squeezed shut with shame.

'I would say, hilariously so,' he replies, honestly.

She opens her eyes, looking dazed at his honesty, before they both burst out laughing.

'You know,' she says, pausing to gulp in some air before adding wistfully, 'I *really* thought I was killing it.' She dissolves into giggles again.

'I know, you did. You looked very happy up there,' he responds softly, with a grin.

'Oh, well. Anyway, my whole life is a much bigger

disaster than what you just saw on that stage,' she had meant to say it like it was some big, funny joke, but the words are more of a heartbroken whisper. Sighing, she squeezes her eyes shut again.

When she opens them a few minutes later, she finds him staring at her curiously.

'What?'

The stage is now filled with a dozen of Khushi's friends, all impossibly gorgeous in designer lehengas, moving effortlessly to '*Chittiyan Kalaiyan*'.

'I don't belong, you know … on that stage, among all these shiny, beautiful people,' she says with a sad smile.

He holds up her face up to his, as he says earnestly, 'You're gorgeous, Pia, and shiny as fuck. I really mean it. This gown is literally blinding me.'

She laughs, despite herself, before the same sadness grips her again. 'Then why is he cheating on me?' she asks in a small voice.

She really didn't mean to.

She blames it on the alcohol and the adrenaline, and the blossoming of some unfair hope inside her that Kabir can somehow fix that sadness.

'Your fiancé?' Kabir asks, and Pia hears a hint of anger in his voice.

'Not my fiancé,' she corrects him softly.

'He's cheating on you?' he asks again.

She nods.

'Well, I can beat him up for you,' he offers.

She laughs again.

'Wait,' he says, a sudden, slow smile spreading across his face. 'Does that mean you're single?'

Pia doesn't reply. *Is she?*

'Because if you are, then I would like to finally do what I have been dying to do all night, or in fact, since the very day I first saw you.'

Pia's toes are already curling at his words, as a slow tingle travels from their tips to the rest of her body, both numbing and electrifying her nerves. The butterflies in her stomach turn feral, flapping up a storm.

'And what is that?' she whispers, unable to tear her eyes from his unrelenting gaze.

His fingers trace her jaw, as his lips touch hers tenderly, tentatively.

But Pia's not in the mood for soft.

A small growl emits from the back of her throat, as she grabs him tighter, turning this into something deeper, darker. Something from which there'll be no turning back.

7

THE WEDDING

Raghav

Her hair tickles his ear, when she brings her dry, cracked lips close to it. Pia's breath is foul when she opens her mouth, as if to devour him. Her voice a terrifying growl, when she says the words –

I know.

He wakes up from the lucid dream to find himself in an empty bed, drenched in five buckets of his own sweat. *She didn't come home last night,* he realizes, followed by a – *Thank God*. The guilt and fear from the dream still hovers in the peripheries of his subconscious, but right now, relief overpowers both those emotions.

He won't worry about Pia's whereabouts. No, not yet. Not when he isn't ready to apologize or be the strange hybrid of villain and knight-in-shining-armour that she constantly expects him to be.

His body is just as unforgiving as his subconscious this morning. He can feel his stomach twist and lurch, threatening to barf while demanding food.

From the corridors, he hears the same old morning cacophony – the vegetable vendor serenading his cabbages and aubergines, the birds screeching in the trees. He stumbles sleepily towards the noise, wondering if Pia has anything in the house besides peanut butter and chicken. As soon as he steps into the kitchen, he does a doubletake and screams loudly, 'Fuck!'

She's sitting on the ground. Strangely still. In the same clothes as last night. She doesn't look like Pia, though, with her mascara smudged, hair dishevelled and matted, and skin two shades paler. Her blue gown is caked in vomit.

She looks feral. 'Jesus, you almost gave me a heart attack,' he mutters. There's an ashtray in front of her. He wasn't aware that she smoked. Or chain-smoked, judging by the ashtray overflowing with cigarette butts.

There's a thick curtain of smoke in the air, as well as the overwhelming stench of tobacco, sweat, vodka and puke, and something else despite the fact that the windows are wide open (through which he can hear the vegetable seller dive into an ominous capsicum and okra raag).

'Are you okay?' he asks her. 'I mean,' he clears his throat, 'where have you been?'

She does not reply. Her eyes are gaping blackholes (for a split second, he thought he saw something more, like a flash of sinister, in there). Save for one arm moving mechanically up and down, bringing the cigarette to her dry, cracked lips, her body is deathly still.

This isn't Pia, he thinks again.

As if to test his theory, he picks up her ashtray and flings it to the floor.

Pia does not flinch. She doesn't even bother turning her head to watch the porcelain shatter into smithereens.

Instead, she continues staring at the wall, flicking the ash on to the floor.

He now recognizes what he had smelt on entering the kitchen. It was the sharp odour of urine.

She's peed herself.

Khushi

'A relapse?' she splutters in rage at Raghav. 'On my wedding day?'

She shoves him out of the way, as she wades across the room in her ten-kilogram lehenga, like a diver navigating the deep underwater and plonks herself in front of the dressing room table mirror.

'Of course!' she sighs.

'Beta, I don't think rolling your eyes is the appropriate response ...' Neeta starts, but stops when she catches her daughter's glowering reflection in the mirror.

Raghav looks visibly uncomfortable, stuck between the two women in the storeroom-turned-bridal-dressing room located a stone's throw away from the garden where the main wedding ceremonies will begin in half an hour. They can hear the celebrations: guests getting desperate for the *varmala*, getting drunk from the open bar and clamouring for the buffet as well as the Bollywood moves they intend to throw on the dance floor. However, the sounds only seem to amplify the tension in the room.

'We'll just get her some more medication and ...' Neeta, the first one to attempt to slice the thick air, says.

'Yes, mom, dope her out as usual,' Khushi rolls her eyes again.

'Is it the mental disorder thing?' the poor, so-out-of-his-depth Raghav ventures.

'Great question!' Khushi hisses like a fanged snake at him. 'Why don't you ask mom? Hey ma! *Is it her mental disorder thing?*' She can barely keep the venom from her voice.

'What do you mean?' a nervous Raghav addresses the ceiling instead.

'I mean that my sister's fucked up. Seriously, how have you never noticed it until now?' Khushi is yelling now, though not nearly as loudly as she would like. Ideally, she would like to be screaming until her lungs collapse.

'Fucked up?'

'Is it some other woman?' Neeta simultaneously demands, invading Raghav's personal space and forcing him to stop inspecting the ceiling and look into her eyes. 'Are you cheating on my daughter?'

'What? No!' he stammers.

'Classic motherly deflection,' Khushi sneers. 'Really, mom? Maybe it has more to do with the guy your daughter was flirting with at my cocktail party.'

'Umm, I'm sorry, but *what now?*' Raghav stutters again, as Neeta holds her hand up in front of his face, attempting to verbally restrain her daughter on the other side of the room. 'Shut up, Khushi!' she warns.

The next thing Raghav knows, Khushi has crept up behind him, and is hissing in his ear, 'She's going to ruin you. Just how she ruined this family!'

'Beta, ignore Khushi,' her mother counters in a jarringly calm tone, grabbing her and escorting her back to the dressing table. 'She is making this about herself.' Khushi can't comprehend how her mother can remain in character while her life is falling apart.

'*Somebody* has to, ma! It's *my* wedding! Yet here we are, still discussing Pia,' she screams again, as her eyes begin to well up.

'Are you crying?' Neeta says, stroking her head. Before Khushi can cling to the maternal softness in her voice, she adds, 'Don't, beta! You'll ruin your makeup.'

This whole family is insane, Khushi realizes, weeping harder now.

'We can do this later …' Neeta is now cooing in an effort to stop the tears. 'I'll handle Pia once she gets here.'

Khushi can barely hear her mother over her own sobs. She places her head in her hands. Neeta motions for Raghav to leave, before bending down to hug her daughter. 'It is your wedding day, beta. And it will be the best day of your life.'

'I just want my mother for *one day*,' she says. Khushi knows she sounds like a child. As she did when she was an actual child. Begging her mother to come play frisbee with her outside. Asking Neeta why she couldn't make it to her Sports Day, her dance recital or her graduation. Knowing the answer each and every time – Pia.

Neeta tightens her hug in apology and offers her vague words as explanation – 'If you knew …'

Khushi pushes her mother away, trembling with rage.

'Again, if I knew. Knew what, ma?' she isn't just yelling now, she's also waving her hands around and pacing the room like in the throes of a nervous breakdown herself. The jingle-jangle sounds of *kaleeras*, *nathnis*, *payals* and earrings fill the room.

'Oh, wait!' she continues. 'Isn't that something, way beyond Dad's and my scope of understanding? It's some strange, messed-up maternal bond between you and her. I hate you more than anything, for making me envy that my whole life!'

'Khushi ...' Neeta begins.

But Khushi has turned towards the mirror again, saving whatever is left of her smokey-eye makeup by dabbing it with a napkin. 'Just so you know,' she says coldly, 'you could have placed your trust in me. With whatever it was ... you know? She's my sister.'

Neeta turns away from her daughter, her eyes tearing up as well.

'But you didn't. All you did was create two monsters: Pia, who can barely wipe her own ass, and me, who can barely love her own sister.'

That's when they hear the rustle of a sari outside the door. And they see Pia slink away.

Pia

She has locked herself in her old bedroom at the other end of the bungalow, with a bottle of vodka she nicked from the bar.

The baraat must be at the gate at this point. She can hear the faint beats of the dhol. In here, with her blouse half-undone and enough vodka to last her the night, she can finally breathe.

She takes a delicate sip, before inhaling the alcohol in desperate gasps.

Soon enough, she hears the voice again … Except it's no longer in her stomach. It echoes across the room.

Thought you'd got rid of all your demons, didn't you?

'One demon,' Pia corrects in a shaky, shattered voice. '*You*,' she adds softly. Her hand is trembling as well, the vodka spilling everywhere.

They could never really kill the demon. Instead, they put it to sleep with an endless supply of pills. It had been lying dormant for fourteen years after her mother found out.

Pia remembers being so confused and terrified. To hear her mother wailing to Dr Agarwal – 'What is wrong with my daughter?' – her nails gripping Pia's shoulders, where they would leave behind angry, red crescent-shaped marks for weeks. 'What is wrong with her?'

She didn't leave Pia's side for two years. Shielding her tightly curled up body every night as the sobs wracked through her frame, she whispered in her steady, maternal voice, 'Shhh … it's gone, it's gone.'

Her father and sister, clueless on the sidelines. Khushi's enraged tantrums: 'It's always about her.'

Poor Khushi. She didn't ask for this. None of them did.

'You're not normal,' her mother had told her, in that

brutally careless yet concerned way of hers. And the words had lodged themselves deep within her.

You're not normal, says the voice – ancient, seductive, womanly. The voice that Pia realizes now is coming out of her mouth.

'I know,' Pia whispers, this time sounding like herself, as she traces a shaky hand down her jaw.

And even though the reflection in the mirror looks like her, Pia knows it is not her.

Oh, but you could be normal, if you really wanted to, it tells her now.

'It's all your fault,' Pia says angrily and defiantly, but she's mesmerized by the reflection that continues to mirror all her actions. By those repulsive yellow eyes webbed with thick red veins.

Don't be like that, it whispers softly to Pia. *I can make it all go away.*

'But I'm happy,' Pia pleads, a tear rolling down her cheek. Or at least as happy as someone like her can be.

The same teardrop falls down the cheek of her alter ego, before its lips start to curl into a hideous smile.

It sends a shiver down Pia's spine, as she begs, 'Please leave.'

She steps away from the mirror and walks towards the door, unlocking it, before it calls out to her teasingly –

Aww. Is it Raghav? Is he the one who makes you 'happy'?

'Stop,' Pia, who is back before the mirror, keeps begging.

Nah, he's too busy fucking … Sonia … was it?

'Please. Stop.'

That Bollywood story he likes telling everyone? Of how he singled you out in the bar that night, the Pia in the mirror laughs, and sighs tauntingly, *Well, he* was *too drunk to remember, wasn't he?*

Pia nods. 'But we promised it would be the last time …'

But you need me now, the demon interrupts her impatiently.

'No, no, I don't. Everything worked out the way it should have. I'm normal now,' she tells herself unconvincingly.

Tell me, Pia. Your parents, they still check up on you every night and every morning, don't they? You'll always be that fucked-up thirteen-year-old in their head! How long will you keep running to Mommy? How long will you pretend to be normal, when you can't even see straight without those … those pills.

The last word was a growl. The reflection is becoming less and less like Pia and more like the demon that it is – ugly, rotting and grey, with peeling skin and gaping wounds, and yellow teeth and eyes.

Come on, it says in that same angry, deafeningly loud growl.

Pia can feel herself shaking at the sight of the demon.

All they do is make you numb!

'I like being numb,' Pia's voice has changed to a thirteen-year-old's. She's terrified yet, as though under a spell, she reaches for the demon in the mirror, raising an arm to touch it. It reaches out to her in the same way. For a moment, it feels like a promise of escape from this life and into oblivion.

Why, the demon hisses and spits at her, *so you don't notice how much you hate looking in the mirror, that 'boyfriend' and yourself?*

Pia is sobbing, as she retreats, gulping down the vodka in her other hand.

The voice becomes gentle, soothing. *Don't cry just yet. You know I've always looked out for you.*

She can feel its grip, which is so tight that she can't breathe, but Pia feels oddly warm. The demon is correct. It has been a part of her entire life and never left her side, even after all these years and all those pills. Somehow, it understands her better than her mother, boyfriend, shrink or even herself.

We're a team, the demon reminds her.

Pia knows that all she has to do is give in. After all, she was never meant to be normal.

At least she tried.

She lets the darkness now engulf her in a choking embrace. But the image of her mother lying awake with her all those nights floods her mind. Pia walks away from mirror.

Bitch, the demon screams. But the remainder of what it is saying is drowned out by Raghav yelling by the door, 'Pia, what are you doing?'

He takes the bottle from her grasp. 'Are you serious? You finished the whole thing?' he thunders. 'They are looking for you downstairs!'

'The demon,' Pia stammers and slurs.

But Raghav has his back to the mirror. He can't see the other Pia smiling back at them.

And so he sighs exasperatedly, running his hands through his hair. 'Look, I don't even know what's got into you lately. Please do me a favour, okay? Just try to be normal.'

Normal. The word echoes in Pia's mind once they are at the *mandap*, but she can't seem to comprehend it. Not when she can see the disapproving glances being shot her way. They've been talking about her. They've *all* been talking about her.

She can read Raghav's thoughts now. *This isn't the girl I fell in love with*, except the voice saying those words is a familiar growl. Her parents are also looking at her strangely – *almost thirty and still living off us.*

The worried look on her mom's face doesn't mask the one thought clearly radiating from her mind: *Mommy. Mommy. Mommy. It never ends with her!*

She looks at Khushi. Her beautiful sister. So pretty. So normal.

'God, Pia,' she exclaims, the only one refusing to hide her disgust for her sister who is currently propped up against Raghav's frame like a puppet. Khushi instead yells, 'Why do you always have to be such a mess?'

The silence that follows is deafening, and then her demon's voice, like a promise, whispers, *It doesn't have to be this way.*

On cue, Pia throws up. There's bile and vodka everywhere, and the dinner she ate an hour ago. She sees the revulsion in everyone's eyes.

Pia is in. It knows Pia is in.

Still, the demon sniggers as it says, *C'mon, Pia. One last ride?*

THREE MONTHS LATER ...

Pia enters the bathroom and peers into the mirror above the basin.

It is as if she's staring at a stranger who bears a passing resemblance to her actual self. Her already too-big eyes, nose and lips that used to be sprawled across her once-round face, now appear clownish and exaggerated. Crammed into the narrow, newly oval space, they fight the arrival of her cheekbones, while her smile threatens to veer off the edge of her sharp jawline.

Her neck is longer now too and, as her gaze travels lower, Pia can see her skin is tautly stretched over her clavicle, which comprises pointed ridges and deep valleys.

She's wearing a tank top and yoga pants that are both see-through and flimsy like second skin, revealing the glaring lack of fat anywhere on her body. It's an outfit she previously wouldn't have dared to wear. The pants would not have made it past her knees anyway.

She does not open the cabinet behind the mirror, where her medication has been sitting for months, untouched.

The stranger in the mirror smiles precariously at her, her shoulders pushed back, spine erect and eyes unwavering with a hint of yellow fire.

8

Pia

When she comes out of the bathroom, she finds Raghav still sleeping in bed, the sheet barely covering his naked body. His arms and legs extended at awkward angles. She walks over and sits next to him, leaning in close to study his face.

He's pretty even with his mouth open in that weird way, the demon sniggers, as Raghav twitches a little in his sleep. *We sure wore him out last night, didn't we?*

'Well, at least one of us was satisfied,' Pia says, grimacing at him.

Well, that is the yakshini curse, for you. We're never satisfied. Not unless we bite their heads off, drink their blood and eat their flesh in the end.

'God, you're gross,' Pia says, her gaze fixed on Raghav. She still can't shake off the feeling of slight disgust, when she sees him. Though his pink lips, long eyelashes and Roman nose are all in perfect proportion – they seem to repel her, instead of turning her on.

He's fluttering those delicate eyelashes slowly now, as he opens his eyes to look at her.

'What the fuck, Pia?' he half-screams in shock.

'What?' she responds, taken aback by his strong reaction and wondering what he just saw in her eyes.

'What are you doing staring at me like that? You look ready to murder me or something. I almost had a heart attack,' he says, dramatically clutching his chest.

'Chill, I was just noticing how long your eyelashes are,' she says, rolling her eyes and then reaching over to caress them with her fingers.

Pia leans in for a long, lingering kiss, before walking over to her wardrobe.

Just like her, it too has undergone a transformation in the last month. For starters, there is no longer anything black or baggy in there. Just a neatly arranged row of figure-hugging dresses, flimsy tops and skinny jeans. Pia had never considered herself fashionable, but that was mainly because she never had the body for it. Now, she spends hours scrolling through Pinterest and Instagram to recreate looks and hunting for bargains at malls. Packages arrive at all hours of the day, following her frequent bouts of online retail therapy – which, incidentally, is the only form of therapy in her life currently.

Nothing beats the thrill of fitting into ridiculously tight, flimsy and sheer dresses. Pia can swear she has a feminine God complex, from lording her skinny body over the rest of the female populace.

Raghav stares at her in the mirror, like a lovesick puppy, as she pulls a cream sari from one of the dresser drawers. It's her mother's, though the tight, black, off-the-shoulder blouse she pairs it with is entirely her handiwork.

She wonders if baring her shoulders is too slutty for a family function. But given that the aforementioned family will be meeting her for the first time after her supposed 'breakdown' at Khushi's wedding, she decides that flaunting her revenge bod is more important than decorum. For added effect, she ties her hair up in a tight chignon.

Raghav continues to watch her, as she drapes the glittery, elaborately embroidered fabric around her frame, allowing her belly button to peek out on purpose.

Her dressing table is now crammed. A slew of makeup products – endless bottles of tinted moisturizers, eye, body and hand creams, mascaras, lipsticks and perfumes – have joined her once-lonely bottle of hair serum and hairbrush.

She takes her time, slathering various creams all over her body before spraying herself with a Dior perfume.

She's generous with her foundation, and goes for a bright pink shade of lipstick.

Then she slips on her high heels and throws on a shawl before turning around to tell Raghav, 'The show is over.'

'You know, I'm really proud of you,' he says as he rolls out of bed and walks towards her. 'The way you're taking care of yourself, your upcoming big artist debut—' his lips graze her neck.

She instantly wiggles out of his embrace.

'I'm getting late,' she admits, apologetically.

'Can't wait to see the final pieces?' he says as she turns to leave, barely noticing how she recoils at his touches.

'Oh, it's a surprise.'

'Just make sure it's not one of those flowers that's actually a vagina or something like that … or anything too feminist. Rohan has developed a strong dislike for that stuff, you know, since #MeToo.'

'Right. But since when do you follow Georgia O'Keeffe?' Pia asks him. She can't help but be impressed.

'What?' Raghav responds.

'Nevermind.' She sighs. 'I've kept Rohan and his douchebag clientele in mind. But, hey, thanks for talking him into doing this,' she says now, gratefully.

He's gone out of his way to help her in the last couple of months, especially after the incident at Khushi's wedding. And it was he who gave her a big break as an artist. It made her feel bad for thinking all those horrible things about him in her head. From how bad he was in bed to how he had the emotional bandwidth of a spoon and the conversation skills of, well, some equally inanimate object. It made the task of reconnecting with him and convincing him to dump Sonia even harder.

'I can't believe he's the unfaithful one,' she cribs as she gets into her car. 'I mean, he can barely satisfy one woman. What business does he have sniffing up another?'

Oh honey, do you think there are better men out there? Because, believe me, I've seen generations of them, and it's really slim pickings. At least this one has top lineage, and is flush in cash and contacts. Even your mother loves him.

'Exactly, that's your red flag, right there!'

She's a smart woman, Pia. It's just a shame about that stick up her ass.

'What about Sonia, then?'

What about her? Let her help herself to your leftovers!

Pia starts the car.

'You know, he still hasn't brought up marriage. I hope to God he's weaning her off, that he is doing something about it – *us*,' she replies, suddenly not in the mood to be playful. 'I don't want to have to step in and take charge. Because if it continues ... we'll have to do something about it.'

Then we'll do something about it, the demon says, soothingly. And just as quickly as it had taken over her, Pia feels the rage leave her, bit by bit, and a quiet, numb calm set in.

All in due time, my love. All in due time.

Neeta

Pia saunters into the house wearing the cream heirloom sari Neeta recognizes as her own, paired with the skimpiest, tartiest blouse she has ever seen. It's black and velvet, low-cut and off-shoulder, and far too short, baring her shoulders, cleavage and stomach wantonly.

'Did you think this was appropriate for my *mata ki chowki*?' Neeta asks disapprovingly, as her daughter dumps her bag on the sofa and asks for a glass of chilled water from Raju.

'You told me that this was an "auspicious" sari,' Pia says, rolling her eyes at her. 'Now, I'm wearing it for your auspicious occasion.'

It was a sari, passed down to Neeta from her mother-in-law, who got it from her own mother-in-law. Neeta had worn it on several significant occasions in her life, including Pia's *naamkaran* and her twenty-fifth wedding anniversary, before gifting it to her own daughter.

'But not with that blouse!' Neeta finally retorts. Her ensuing rant is interrupted by her sister-in-law Bubbly and the rest of the aunty squad that has just wandered into the living room.

'Pia! You're less than half your size!' exclaims Bubbly, followed by Kamlesh. '*Kaise* reduce *kiya itna*!'

Then Reshma and Parmeet jump in with – 'Keto? Atkins? Some special dietician?'

All the plump fifty-somethings, dressed in similar sparkling saris, with elaborate blow-dried hairdos, have gathered around her now, looking up at her with fervent devotion, as if she's a guru poised to reveal to them the elusive secrets of life and weight loss.

Pia flashes them a benign smile, as she self-deprecatingly says, 'It's a combination of yoga and, well, stress.'

'Rubbish. You're radiant! *Haaye*, why doesn't stress hit us the same way,' laments Bubbly, before resuming her interrogation, 'So, where are you doing yoga?'

Before Pia can respond, Khushi appears, also a vision in a bridal red salwar kameez with the traditional thick red and white bangles covering each of her arms. When she spots Pia, she greets her with the same shocked expression as Neeta.

'Pia! You're so *tinnny* now. Even skinnier than me!' Khushi screeches, and Neeta detects the slightest hint of jealousy in her tone. 'And that blouseeee! Are you trying to seduce the pundit or what?'

Despite the slight, her elder daughter grins, revelling in the title of the 'Skinniest Bhandari'.

'I don't stand a chance – not with the way you're giving competition to Mata in that outfit,' she then replies snidely, referring to Khushi's hyper-red, blingy, post-marital avatar.

Not that they'd ever got along, but Neeta has felt that Khushi and Pia's relationship has become even more strained in the past few months, since the latter's claws have emerged.

'Stop squabbling you two,' Neeta says, ushering them both out to their sprawling garden, now covered with a tent. A larger-than-life idol of the goddess (whose bright red sari is quite similar to Khushi's get-up, Neeta begrudgingly admits to herself) beams down at her audience as a man dressed in a white kurta-pyjama with a gold-embroidered red dupatta tied around his forehead, is bellowing devotional numbers set to the tune of the latest Bollywood tracks. He gestures to the idol frantically, as he sings a Mata-ized version of a Bipasha Basu number.

'*Beedi Jalai Le*-jagrata remix?' Pia rolls her eyes at Neeta as she walks away. 'And you thought my blouse was too scandalous?'

'She looks exactly like you, Neeta. When you were a thirty-something!' Parmeet yells to her over a devotional track set to the tune of a Katrina Kaif song. But Neeta doesn't see it anymore – the resemblance. She's a far cry from Pia's in-your-face, glam version today, dressed in a simple, peach *chikankari* suit, with minimal jewellery and makeup.

Even the way Pia walks seems different, Neeta notices, the unsettling feeling in her tummy growing by the second. There's an added sway to her hips, an exaggerated femininity in her gestures.

That face, plastered in makeup, is so hard and angled now. The weight loss has rendered her so completely unrecognizable, that for the first time in their lives, Neeta has no idea what Pia is thinking.

The thought sends a chill down Neeta's spine.

*

'I hope you're eating enough. I am just a bit concerned. Our bodies … they aren't supposed to be this skinny,' she tells Pia, as they clean up after the guests.

'Our bodies?' Pia repeats, rolling her eyes. 'Mom, you need to stop treating us as if we are a single entity. Besides, I'm fine.'

'How much do you weigh now?' Neeta asks.

Pia can't stop beaming when she replies, 'Forty-five kilos – it's perfectly within the healthy range, ma!'

Neeta remembers the time when she had brought her own weight down to forty-five kilos, when she suffered from an eating disorder without even realizing it. It was right after she had given birth to Pia.

In the grip of postpartum depression, what had affected her the most was how different she looked after giving birth (and she had never truly looked the same). Angry red blotches of eczema scarring her skin. Her limbs and features doubly swollen. Her body thrice its usual size. The post-op slashes and scars across her belly. She couldn't bear to look into the mirror for several months. And so, in a bid to control her body and channel her self-hatred, she had taken to eating only one apple a day.

It wasn't until she fainted in the middle of her routine household chores one day and awoke to find Dr Agarwal and her husband by her bedside, looking sad, afraid and disappointed that she realized she needed to stop.

'Your child needs you, Neeta,' Dr Agarwal had told her calmly, jolting her back to reality.

As much as Pia would like to deny it, she has inherited her mother's genes abundantly, including her pear-shaped lineage, though her frame has now shrunk by a considerable extent.

'Didn't you want me to lose weight? You're the one who nagged me to go to Zumba, spinning and "dancersize" classes and taught me how to count my calories. What's the problem now?'

'I just wanted you to be healthy,' Neeta says helplessly. 'You've lost too much weight too quickly. I hope you're eating well and not pushing yourself overly hard. Forty-five kilos is very little, beta. You're looking so emaciated!'

'Emaciated? I am sure Bubbly bua would disagree with you.'

'Well, Bubbly bua is an idiot.'

'Cut it out, ma. This constant criticism is getting exhausting. What's the problem now? My life is back on track. My weight is under control, and I am painting again. I am *this* close to getting engaged. Why are you getting so upset with me?'

Defeated, Neeta switches to a new line of offence.

'You rarely call me anymore, and Dr Agarwal says he hasn't seen you in two months.'

'I've been busy. You know, I have an exhibition of my paintings coming up …'

'But Pia, you can't skip your appointments.'

'And yet I seem to be doing great.' Pia rolls her eyes.

'For now, beta. But with your history. With your condition …'

Pia exits the living room and asks the driver to bring her car out, but Neeta grabs her by the arm just as she's about to enter the driveway. Holding it so tight she's sure to leave behind a thick bruise, she looks Pia in the eye and roars, 'I am your mother. When I tell you to do something, you BLOODY WELL LISTEN TO ME!'

For a moment, she can see the familiar terror in her daughter's eyes.

Still, if it really came down to it, what could Neeta possibly do to stop Pia from hurtling down that self-destructive path again?

'Alright. I'll make an appointment for Sunday,' Pia says in a small voice.

Neeta is unsure whether this is a win, however. In fact, as she watches Pia drive away in her bright yellow Volkswagen Beetle, she isn't sure at all how long it will be before she completely loses her daughter.

Pia

Are you certain you want to eat that? the voice appears to taunt her, as she fiddles with a burger on her plate the next morning.

'I'm an emotional eater, and I need the carbs.'

A moment on the lips, forever on the hips, darling, it reminds her, ignoring her whining.

'You know, I hate how you always sound like her,' Pia snaps at the demon. Finding that she's lost her appetite, she pushes the plate away.

You know, you don't have to see the psychiatrist today, right? She doesn't control you anymore.

'Bullshit, she'll always control me, and eventually choke me to death with the damn umbilical cord.'

Well, then, it's time to break free and ditch that therapy snoozefest. All those pills he prescribed you have done is numb you. And you know you're of no use to me that way.

'I know,' Pia says, chewing on her nails instead of the burger and gazing into the distance.

Your mom doesn't understand you, Pia. She's also been holding you back! Look at how far we've come in the last month!

Pia sighs and dumps the uneaten burger in the dustbin.

'I can't dodge this session and you know it,' she says, dusting off her hands. 'She'll make my life hell if I don't. Let's just get it over with.'

*

'Your mother's concerned,' Dr Agarwal tells her. Just being in his office again makes Pia feel depressed.

Shouldn't it be the other way around?

'That's shocking, because she's the very picture of cool and calm otherwise, isn't she?' Pia comments sarcastically.

Dr Agarwal gives her his usual, empty stare.

'She fears you might not be taking your medicines,' he ploughs on insufferably.

'I am doing fine,' she says, trying to evade his question. 'Better than fine, actually. I think I am doing great.'

'We've been through all of this before, Pia. You not taking your medication; you feeling fine, great even. That's why we know that this high you're feeling … it isn't real. You're going to crash, and when you do, the low will be just as low,' he warns.

His tone, however, does not intimidate or scare her. Instead his righteousness and condescension make her insides flare with rage – rage that has been building up inside her all this time, only she didn't have a voice to express it. She finds herself suddenly unconcerned about the consequences or how her temper or insubordination might come back to bite her.

She keeps her voice low, continuing in the same sarcastic tone, 'You know, what I don't get? How she and you have managed to pull off this con for all these years. In fact, I might even admire you for it.'

'What are you going on about, Pia?'

'You know what I am talking about. You know who the sick one really is!'

He actually has the gall to still look confused.

'How do you sleep at night knowing what you've done to me … knowing what *she* has done to me! Or maybe, you even enjoy it. You get some sick feeling of schadenfreude watching poor, helpless Pia get pushed around,' she continues. 'Watching me mess up my life while drugged out of my mind, dancing around like her little puppet …'

She lets out a small, phoney laugh.

'You're not here to cure me. You're just here to enable … whatever sick game she's playing with me.'

'Pia, this is why you need your medicine. Is this the voice? Is it telling you all these things? Making you believe this is all a conspiracy?'

Pia finds herself tearing up at his apathy.

'I fucked up *once*. I made a mistake *once*. Does that exempt me from living a normal life, forever? How long will you both keep doing this to me?'

'Pia, we just want you to be healthy, to be yourself.'

'No,' Pia shakes her head. 'You don't get it. She *wants* me to be sick. She *needs* me to be sick. Because it's my sickness that feeds hers.'

9

Kabir

He walks into the pub, which is modelled after an abandoned warehouse, with bare brick walls and massive copper pipes snaking the ceiling, and is as shocked to see Pia standing there, as she is to see him.

'I am sorry, is that why you never called me back after our one night together all those months ago? Because you were stranded on some island like Tom Hanks in *Cast Away*?' Kabir is only half-joking. Pia seriously looks as if she hasn't had a proper meal since that night.

That isn't to say she looks bad. She is stunning, in fact, dressed in a tight-fitting yellow jumpsuit that barely covers all of her dangerous parts. Combined with her sweeping eyeliner and bright red lipstick, it is making his mind wander past doors he had locked after she had shut him out following their one-time and one-time-only hook-up.

Pia still seems taken aback by his presence, and at the words coming out of his mouth. So, she shoots him a look of confusion. 'What?'

As usual, he deflects the situation with more jokes, 'I

didn't realize you were literally ghosting me, by becoming a ghost yourself.'

But Pia isn't amused. In fact, she is looking even more confused now, with an 'are you okay or did you hurt your head?' expression on her face.

'It's the weight. You've lost a lot of it,' he finally admits, feeling a bit stupid.

'Right,' Pia replies, smiling politely. 'And, anyway, what are you doing here?'

'It's Friday evening, and this is a pub, so? Gardening, from the looks of it.'

'Ha ha.' Pia gives him a sidelong glance. 'I was just wondering, since this is an invite-only event ...'

'And I am but a lowly peasant ...' he finishes for her, raising an eyebrow.

This time, she lets out a genuine laugh. 'Come on, you know I didn't mean it like that,' she says, punching his arm. 'You just ... don't move around in the same circles as I do, so ...'

'Well, I do like coming out from the squalor now and then to see how the one per cent lives,' he replies. Then, leaning in closer, he whispers in mock amazement, 'I mean, there's a champagne fountain in the middle of the room. There are lobsters and caviar on the menu!'

'Actually, that is Aquitaine caviar, from southwest France. My boyfriend sourced it.'

'Wow.'

'Yup, I know it's pretty cool. The thing about caviar is that it needs to be stored at a cool temperature, but not too cold ...' she's rambling now.

'No, I mean, wow, you're still with him. You know, after the cheating and ...'

'And our one night of passion?' Pia smiles mischievously, taking a sip of her wine, while she peers at him from over the glass. Even her nails, he notices, are French manicured now.

He realizes that the Pia standing in front of him is a different one. The fact both intimidates and arouses him.

Great, all the doors in his mind are fully open, allowing him complete access to the memory he had buried deep in his subconscious, leading to strange dreams about him entangled in the forests of her curly hair or his balls growing a giant blue before turning into disgusting raisins and then withering away and eventually falling off his body.

'I'm sorry,' he says, clearing his throat a bit self-consciously. 'You look very different.'

'And? Do you like the new and improved Pia?' she teases, leaning back so he can take it all in, which he does, right down to her glittery platform heels and that delicious smell – floral yet sharp – that always seems to emanate from rich South Delhi women.

'Well, I like the cocky you,' he says, putting on his trademark charm, which Pia has always been completely immune to.

'But,' he lets it hang in the air for a while, for added effect.

'Oh, there's a but?' she says in that same new cocky way of hers. A way he wishes he didn't find so simultaneously seductive and irritating.

'You're like … proper South Delhi bourgeoisie now,' he replies.

'And does that intimidate the East Delhi boy in you?' she retorts challengingly.

He laughs. 'Touché, but I think I liked the older Pia a tad more.'

'Because the new one won't let you get in her pants,' she teases him again.

'Oh please, you'd take them off in a second, if I actually try to. Or maybe ten to fifteen … the jumpsuit looks a bit tricky,' he replies, holding her gaze.

She shakes her head, looking away with a slight smile.

That's when he realizes it's still there – the chemistry. It crackles, electrifying the air between them.

He can swear she's a little breathless too, when she finally whispers, 'So, what's holding you back?'

After considering her question for a second, he is still unsure. He can't decide if it's her coldness, the boyfriend or the fact that he might not really like this new 'let them eat cake' version of her – not that any of that would stop him right now, this very second. It's all he wants to do. It's all his body is screaming for anyway. But he chooses to tell her the real reason instead: 'I just … I don't want you to think I'm … *easy*.' He almost winces as he says it.

She laughs, before leaning in till her lips hover over his, 'Too bad. I was hoping for easy.'

That's when he knows for sure, that their second night of passion is about to begin.

Pia

'That was both, idiotic and dangerous,' she says, as they stumble back into the pub. 'And a mistake,' she adds, hoping to God there are no CCTV cameras in the parking lot. What was she thinking? Hooking up with him in his car, while her boyfriend was right here inside.

It was thrilling, if you ask me, the demon's whispering now, and Pia asks it to please shut up.

'It's alright. I am pretty irresistible,' Kabir smiles and says.

Unfortunately, he is. Pia sighs as she takes a second to appreciate how good he looks tonight in a simple white shirt and blue jeans. His careless hair and dimpled smile do things to her again. So, she isn't sure why she's snapping at him and saying things like, 'Can you not crack a silly joke for five seconds?'

'Hey, Pia. Everyone has been looking for you,' Raghav says, from right behind them and Pia jumps a foot high at the sound of his voice.

Wipe that guilty look off your face, Pia. Stop staring at the ceiling and look straight into his eyes. I mean, this is Lying 101.

'Raghav, hey! I just … why?' she blabbers, as Kabir extends his hand and says in formal greeting, 'Great caviar, man.'

'Thanks, bro,' Raghav says, shaking his hand, puzzled by the words coming out of both their mouths.

Despite herself, Pia finds herself ten seconds away from laughter at this ridiculous scene.

'Raghav, this is Kabir, an ex-colleague. Now, why on earth is everyone looking for me?'

'Your painting has found a buyer already.'

'Shut up!' she says, punching her boyfriend in the arm in surprise.

'He's offering a lakh, but I think we can negotiate for more. Also, he just happens to own an art gallery in Hauz Khas, where he exhibits the works of emerging artists, so … how does next month sound?'

'Are you serious?' Pia yells, wrapping Raghav in a tight hug, saying 'thank you' over and over.

When they finally break apart, she sees that Kabir is still standing there, staring at them with an odd expression on his face.

'Would you like to see it?' Pia asks him awkwardly, and he just shrugs in response, resigned to his sudden demotion to third wheel.

As they all make their way to the centre of the pub, she compares and contrasts the two men. Next to Kabir, Raghav's exaggerated attempts at being the alpha male look almost comical. He's wearing a tight black shirt today, which means that it was chest day at the gym, along with blue jeans. Even his gait, in comparison to Kabir's lazy and casual one, feels a bit ridiculous, with the top of his arms hiked up to make it look like he's about to break into the robot dance step, and his chest puffed up like a male frigatebird's during mating season.

When they reach the wall, Pia's pleasantly surprised to see three people already standing there and observing it.

'It's brilliantly terrifying,' says one.

'Very oriental,' adds the other.

Staring at them is a beautiful Japanese woman, standing

still in the middle of an icy blizzard. Her violet eyes are disproportionately large on her petite face, similar to the ratio of her breasts to the rest of her body. Around her, her white hair flows frenetically. She's wearing a flimsy white kimono, the same colour as the white ice that surrounds her. The expression on her face, though, can be interpreted as helpless or hostile, depending on who is looking at it. Her one arm is outstretched, making it look as if she's crying out for help, or perhaps a second away from drawing you into the dark blizzard with her, again, depending on how one chooses to look at it.

'That's Yoki-unna, a Japanese snow demon. She traps lost male travellers and sucks their lives out of them. According to some other legends, she also drinks their blood,' Pia whispers to Kabir.

'Wow, that's hardcore,' says Kabir.

'You swore to me you wouldn't paint anything weirdly feminist,' Raghav's saying now. 'This *feels* like it might be. The whole female demons drinking men's blood thing might trigger Rohan. He has, like, six #MeToo cases against him so far.'

'He thought it was Manga,' she shrugs.

Turning to Kabir, she says, 'I am a little obsessed with demons.'

'I'd love to see more of your work some time,' Kabir says, staring at her meaningfully.

'I guess, then you have a date with the demonesses next month,' Raghav smiles, doing that weird half-hug, half-hand-holding, semi-violent-back-patting thing he does every time he wants to express affection towards another man.

10

Khushi

'Wow, this place is gorgeous!' Pia says, with a low whistle, as she steps inside the second floor of the GK-2 kothi, which is now her sister's marital abode.

'*Merci*,' Khushi smiles at her sister. 'I did it up pretty much by myself. I could totally be an interior designer now.'

She watches Pia take in her surroundings – an open-floor apartment reminiscent of NYC penthouses. She'd broken down two walls to turn them into giant windows, while the others are painted a subtle grey, one covered in sprawling canvases of contemporary works – the expensive kind – which, she's sure, Pia the artist would appreciate. But she doesn't seem as impressed as Khushi had expected. In fact, she can swear she heard Pia mutter something along the lines of 'Jackson Pollock, of course' under her breath.

'It's an original. Kaushal wants to invest in contemporary art ... It's a valid form of currency now, you know?' Even as Khushi says it, she feels a little embarassed. Like she's pandering to her sister, of all people. But she can't stop herself.

'I was hoping you could do a piece for the wall as well. Like a portrait of me and Kaushal. And, Butters! I am pretty sure I won't be able to afford a Pia Bhandari original after next month!' Khushi laughs nervously as she says this.

On hearing his name being called, her little pug comes bolting towards them out of nowhere, crashing comically at Pia's feet. Exhausted, he lays there, licking her toes.

'That pose, right there!' Khushi laughs again. 'What do you say?'

Pia looks at her with an indecipherable expression, before finally replying, 'You know, I am not a portrait artist.'

It's the disdain and condescension in her sister's voice that makes Khushi snap, 'I know, it was a *joke*. And even if it wasn't, I'm sure it would be a welcome break from all the morbid demon stuff you paint.'

She's never heard Pia be so condescending before, and it feels like a messed-up, role-reversal game they are playing, all of a sudden.

Pia sighs, 'Forget I said that, Khushi. I think I just really need a glass of wine!'

As she fetches one for her sister, Khushi can't help but still feel bitter. Maybe because Pia is supposed to be the perennially messy one in the family, and she doesn't seem all that messy anymore.

In fact, tonight, she looks gorgeous, dressed in a knee-length nude-coloured dress that is tailored to her slight curves. She's so much smaller now, like a miniaturist piece of contemporary artwork herself. High cheekbones, a long prominent nose, full, round lips and glittering eyes. Her hair is pulled back into a tight bun at the nape. She looks like the very portrait of restraint and dignity.

Khushi flinches as she sees their reflection together in the gold-tinted mirror above the dining table.

It is not that she doesn't look good tonight in an emerald green sari and sleeveless, turtle-necked gold blouse. Her makeup is flawless, and her hair perfectly styled in light beach waves. But next to her sister, for the first time in her life, she feels – plain.

Pia's distracted gaze flits around, half-heartedly taking in all the decor that Khushi had spent months working on.

This upsets Khushi even more, seeing as how she had choreographed her housewarming party in a way so that she'd walk each guest through the wall of contemporary art, then the open kitchen, then the living room filled with plush sofas and mahogany tables and thick, cushioned chairs and cherry wood bookshelves filled with law tomes she had spent months sourcing. They would pause there, as the guests browsed through the various leatherbound titles, marvelling at her collection and her exquisite taste in decor. Then, they'd go to the bedrooms, which were decorated in soft colours like mauve and beige, with carpets you could sink your feet into, beds and settees that felt like soft, velvet quicksand, and throw pillows and rugs strewn about everywhere, spelling carelessness and comfort.

Pia, however, has had enough and sinks into a sofa.

Khushi has no choice but to plonk down next to her.

An awkward silence follows. Khushi isn't sure how to speak to her sister anymore. Even in the past, they never seemed to have anything in common. However, now, there's an added edge to this relationship. As though there's a new fight over who is the alpha sister – when the answer in the past was always Khushi.

She had the better grades, the looks, the personality, and then the career, and the husband. Though at the time she had never felt smug or in any way self-congratulatory about those things, she feels weirdly competitive about her spot now. The earlier-Khushi would have graciously told people, 'Come on, this isn't a race. Pia is lovely in her own ways', but the new Khushi suddenly doesn't want to let go of the status and the perks of being the better, hotter sister.

Already, she can see the other guests craning their necks to get a good look at this Pia, treating her like some kind of a movie star for simply dropping a few kilos.

She can't figure out how her sister always manages to steal the show, with minimal effort.

'Where's Raghav?' Khushi asks, and Pia shrugs, 'Working late again.'

'All good between you two?'

'Never been better,' Pia says warily.

Khushi nods, realizing that Pia is no longer as vulnerable as she once was. She doesn't know why she's even trying to get to her, or why she says what she says next.

'So, who was the other guy then?'

Khushi knows she has gone too far with this one – it's a surprisingly bitchy move, even for her, yet she can't seem to help it.

'Which guy?' She senses the warning in Pia's tone, but it doesn't deter her.

'The one you were with at my cocktail party?' Khushi can tell she has struck a nerve from the way Pia narrows her eyes. Better still, it's the moment their mother joins them.

With a small smile, Khushi continues, 'Wait, is that what the breakdown was all about?'

'Who is this guy now?' her mother is asking Pia, making her sigh in frustration. Neeta then touches her daughter's arm, asking in concern, 'Beta, is everything okay with Raghav?'

'Of course, it is, ma.'

'What about that girl, Sonia?'

'Who Sonia?' Khushi interjects, her ears perking up.

'Mom, stop it! And why are you so interested in my personal life all of a sudden, Khushi? You haven't bothered to call me once in the last three months.'

Because you ruined my wedding, Khushi wants to scream, but she chooses to remain silent instead. Their mother seems to be doing all her work anyway.

'Just get married, you two. I don't know how long you're going to go round and round,' Neeta sighs.

'She's right, you know,' Khushi adds, glad to resume her role as the condescending, holier-than-thou sister once again. 'It's high time.'

'Seriously?' Pia says incredulously. 'What are you so

smug about, Khushi? The fact that you've always chosen the most boring, safe and unoriginal path in life? Or is it because you bagged a boring accountant and are some kind of a trophy wife now?'

Her voice grows even louder, as she continues.

'Your life makes me want to throw up. Your god-awful, Pinterest-inspired apartment, and your uninspiring, douchey friends, make me want to throw up. You're all the same people, living the same life, doing the same jobs, having the same conversations, over and over and over again – it makes me want to tear the hair out of my scalp!' she exclaims, literally clutching at her hair, till her bun comes undone, and her messy curls tumble down across her shoulders.

'Pia, stop it!' her mother is saying now.

Sensing all eyes in the room on her, Pia gets up, and flings her handbag over her shoulder as she walks towards the front door.

She's almost about to yank it open, when she changes her mind. Turning around, she walks towards the bar and grabs a glass of red wine. 'You know what, instead of a personal portrait, here's my gift to you.'

Khushi watches Pia's sharp features now twist into a horrible, Picasso-like arrangement, as she flings the wine all over the apartment's newly painted grey wall.

There are audible gasps from every guest in the house and a loud shriek from their mother.

'Now, *that*'s contemporary art,' Pia says, before stomping out.

Khushi knows she should be upset. But instead, she

wants to laugh. She can't believe she thought she could be bested by her sister.

The perennially messy one.

Pia

'That felt … amazing,' she says, as she finally reaches home. Taking off her shoes, she flings them to one side of the room, and heads to the kitchen.

With all that adrenaline surging through her veins, she suddenly feels ravenous.

Right?

'I mean, it was *cathartic*.'

You've tasted blood now, and I like it.

'Of course, it wasn't very nice of me, and you know mom will be calling up tomorrow and making me pay for this, but …' Pia says, as an afterthought, as she starts constructing a four-storey sandwich for herself as reward.

Nice is boring, darling! I like you better when you're scandalizing the family in deep neck blouses and flinging wine on walls, and shacking up with Mr Sexy Ex-Colleague. Speaking of the devil … I think it's time for another booty call, how about you?

'*No!* I am on my way to getting engaged to Raghav. This feels like an unnecessary complication,' she argues. Besides that's a hole she doesn't intend to fall into. There's a reason he's got his way with most women in that office. The messy hair, the tall lanky frame, the dimples, the charm – it's all a bit too much.

Though, out here in the safety of her kitchen, with

no witnesses in sight, she can finally admit to herself – that he was the best sex of her life.

Exactly! Raghav's having his fun with Sonia. Why should you sit here like a sati savitri *the whole time? Why don't you get to have a side-piece as well? Where is your feminism now!*

'Stop manipulating my feminism to justify your perverted sense of fun. Also, Kabir doesn't want to be a side-piece. You heard what he said,' she says, licking the Thousand Island salad dressing off her fingers.

Does that matter? Come on, give Raghav a taste of his own medicine. Maybe that's what has been missing from this game!

'And Kabir?'

He's a big boy. He'll get over it.

She grabs the sandwich and is about to take a giant bite of it, when the demon roars, *Pia!*

'What?'

I thought we discussed this – no carbs after 5 p.m.!

Neeta

She rushes to Dr Agarwal's office the very next day after Khushi's housewarming to talk to him about what happened, but he has no solutions to offer her.

'She still hasn't seen me, and she is definitely not taking her medicines,' Dr Agarwal tells her. 'But we can't force her to either.'

'What do you recommend, then?' Neeta asks.

'Staying on the sidelines and observing are the best we can do for the time being.'

'And what if she gets out of control again, like the

last time?' Neeta asks, baffled as to how he can be so nonchalant about this.

'Then we'll have to get her admitted to a proper institution, Neeta.'

'Why can't we do that now?'

Dr Agarwal lets out an impatient sigh.

'I feel like we have discussed this before, Neeta. That the laws surrounding involuntary admissions are quite strict. Besides, apart from this incident, she seems to be doing quite well ...'

He's making her sound paranoid, Neeta realizes. Like she's some zealous, overprotective mother.

'She's starving herself. Every time I see her, she has lost even more weight,' she argues.

'Then you have grounds to get her treated for anorexia, Neeta, depending, of course, on whether the doctors agree with you.'

His tone, again, seems to imply that it's Neeta, who needs help.

But she can't seem to stop. 'So, what do we do then? Wait until she does something horrible again? You know exactly what she is capable of, doctor!'

'That was fourteen years ago – and it wasn't exactly grounds for admitting her into a psychiatric institution either,' Dr Agarwal replies.

'She heard voices in her head. She thought a demon was talking to her, for God's sake!' Neeta's voice is almost pleading as she reminds him. 'Didn't you see what it made her do the last time?'

'Do you have any reason to believe it's back?'

'Of course, it is back! That's what I've been trying to explain to you!' Neeta yells frustratedly.

'Has she mentioned it, or have you heard her talking to it?'

'No, because we hardly ever meet or talk! She is shutting me out of her life!' Neeta exclaims.

Dr Agarwal shakes his head again.

'Neeta, then have you considered that this may just be your own anxieties acting up? I could prescribe you something for it. You look like you haven't been sleeping well either,' he says kindly, in the same tone he uses on his patients. It infuriates her further.

'How about you figure out what we do about Pia? Because that is what will help me sleep at night,' she rages at him, before storming out.

11

Pia

As her art debut looms closer, she feels like she's slowly but surely losing her mind.

She is standing now in front of the pieces she thought were finished, but she can't stop herself from painting over them. Using harsher strokes and deeper colours, as if she wants the demons to literally breathe and move like they were real. To step right out of the canvas. To come alive and tear her, and everyone who ever set their eyes on them, apart.

When she runs out of space on the canvases, she begins scribbling on scraps of paper, filling up the room with thousands of haphazardly drawn images. The face scrawled over and over again. A woman with big, haunting eyes. Except she keeps thinking the eyes aren't big enough. She needs to draw them larger. And she has to keep doing it until she gets it right, even if that means drawing the same eyes, over and over again, till dawn. When she's done, she locks up all evidence of her growing insanity and leaves it behind in the storeroom, which is off limits to everyone.

She feels this same way about Kabir and can't help but drive to his East Delhi flat every other night. Each time she's in his home, which is really a *barsati*, with a makeshift roof and crumbling furniture, she tells herself it would be the last time. But she finds herself growing fidgety in the days that follow. The closer they get, the more he intimidates her. Turns out, being a photographer for TOTT was only a side-gig. His main ambition is to save the world or something. His shelves are stacked with books by Marx and Chomsky, as well as anthologies on philosophy and ancient Greek plays. She had tried to dismiss him as a wannabe JNU activist, but he appears to care. He is always out protesting alongside farmers and against the illegal razing of minority communities' homes.

'It's like you feel things on a deeper level …' she had said to him once.

'So do you, your art – it tries to say something,' he'd told her.

She shook her head, replying softly, 'We both know how navel-gazey I can be. Just like everyone I know in my life. We're always looking inwards. I wish I could …' She trailed off.

'Sometimes, I think you feel you're trapped in your world, your body, your brain. You're not.'

If he only knew who or what you really are, the demon giggled in her brain.

She realizes that all of this is only fracturing her relationship with Raghav further. She can barely look at him anymore. She can't listen to him talk either. Every time he opens his mouth, she wants to yell at him to shut up. She wants to kick and bite herself free every time he approaches the bed.

'What is happening to me?'

You're falling in love with a broke hippie, the demon replies, its voice sounds bored and full of contempt. *Snap out of it. We have work to do.*

Pia knows Raghav will propose to her any time now, and she shudders at the prospect of spending the rest of her life with him.

But the thought of spending the rest of your life in Kabir's hovel doesn't make you shudder?

'At least I love him.'

Oh, you love him. I'm sorry, my bad. Of course, you do! You know, that's what you guys can eat for breakfast, lunch and dinner – love! That's what you can pay rent with. It's all you need to survive. And that's what you can tell your mother, when you finally introduce her to him – ma, I'm in love!

She hears the demon chuckle, as she says next: *You know, what? Go ahead and do it. It'll be fun watching that expression on your mother's face when you tell her you broke up with Raghav to go live in an ashram in the Himalayas. That's what he wants to do, right, eventually?*

'He may have mentioned it once or twice,' Pia shrugs, biting her lower lip.

It's delusional. You know what, you're fucking naive, Pia. All this 'I don't wanna be tied down in one place', 'I don't want baggage', etc., that's fuckboy-speak for commitment-phobic. How the fuck will he commit to you if he can't commit to a fucking job or a fucking place?

And you honestly believe that you can let go of the golden spoon in your mouth? You can barely spend more than three hours in his third-world apartment!

'So, what do I do?' Pia asks the voice in her head, listlessly dabbing more colours onto the canvases, feeling trapped in some kind of purgatory, torn between two lives.

Raghav is bound to find out eventually, if she continues like this. She isn't as good as him at cheating. She finds herself constantly messing up dates, timings and excuses, and leaving behind all sorts of traces.

On the other hand, Kabir's patience is wearing thin as well. He has already issued her ultimatums to make her choice or let him go.

'What the fuck do I do?' she screams again, tearing at her hair.

Come on, Pia. You already know the answer to that question, don't you?

*

Raghav is pouting again. This time, in a mirror covering the wall at the entrance to the art gallery.

Pia's about to make some snide comment, when he jerks her to his side, motioning with his chin towards the mirror.

'Look at us,' he says to her, with a grin. 'And look at you, babe. Tonight, you own this place!'

For a moment, Pia is hypnotized by the reflection they cast in it. The couple staring back at them makes her want to laugh, and then scream, 'That's not us!'

But it is them. That's him in a fitted black shirt and trousers looking deliciously hot, and that's her in a tight, short red dress with six-inch strappy heels, smiling coyly, with his arm wrapped around her slim waist. Pia lets Raghav navigate her to the centre of the room with wooden-panel flooring and stark white walls covered in her art, which people are standing in front of and analysing over hors d'oeuvres.

They walk past the canvases, taking in her entire series, starting with the Scandinavian forest demon Huldra. She's drawn her as a cross between a forest nymph and a terrifying monster.

A small wooden board underneath the painting reads: 'Seductive and stunning, the Huldra has a face so exquisite, you almost don't notice the tail of a cow peeking out from underneath her dress, or the fact that as she peers at you from over her shoulder, her entire back is covered in bark. According to the legend, until you notice these two aspects, her beauty will seduce and enslave you till she sucks the very life force out of you.'

Then the world's oldest female spirit – the Sumerian demon Lilith – painted entirely in the nude, with her hands bound and two enormous horns poking out from each side of her head.

'Known to have an untameable sexual appetite, which she uses to birth demons, Lilith is believed to be Adam's first wife, even before Eve, who he shunned after she refused to be anything but his equal. Her hands are bound to keep her from unleashing her sexuality and chaos onto the world.'

Then there's the Caribbean La Diablesse, whom Pia has painted with milky skin, her bosom spilling out of the flowing medieval dress, but her face covered entirely by a hat.

'A human who made a deal with the devil to become a demon. If you look closer, you'll see a sliver of her face – hideously scarred and disfigured. Look closer still, and you might also notice the cow hoof peeking out from under her dress. She has a reputation of luring men deep into the woods, where they meet their deaths.'

Next is the Caribbean Mama Dglo. Above the water, Pia has depicted her as a stunning siren, with glistening skin and long, lustrous hair. However, the majority of the canvas is taken up by her massive, coiled anaconda tail, which is submerged from the waist down.

Her name translates to 'mother of water' in English, and she is known to punish men who wreck the earth's forests and rivers by marrying them for several lives.

And, lastly, the Yakshini – drawn exactly in Pia's likeness, but with larger breasts and even wider hips, barely covered by her flimsy, almost transparent robe.

'The yakshinis are both feared as demons for their sexuality and worshipped as goddesses of fertility, at the same time. But it really depends on how you see them. They have been vilified for unleashing disasters and terrors on humanity, but also praised for protecting them. Portrayed as shapeshifters, who feed on the flesh and blood of men, they are also regarded as wish-granters, though it's argued that they only feed your desires in this life so you may suffer in the next ones.'

Boy, we really put ourselves out there with this one. You think they'll notice?

'Nah, none of these people will notice things that are right under their nose,' Pia scoffs.

She finds herself wandering away from the crowd and the noise, to the back gate of the gallery, where she takes out a cigarette.

'Look at you,' she hears a familiar voice say. 'That dress is simply ravishing!' it continues, before adding, 'You know, mental breakdowns really suit you.'

'Hey, Clara,' Pia says, smiling. Dressed in an off-shoulder, body-hugging, floral dress, with her thick black hair pinned back in a semi-beehive hairdo – Clara looks stunning as usual. Taking out a cigarette of her own, she lights it with Pia's, before exhaling, and pointing it towards the gallery behind them.

'You've made it,' she says, grinning widely and giving her a side hug. 'I mean, those pieces inside? My mind is blown!'

'Thanks,' Pia grins.

'Could totally relate to … the Yakshini, was it? Man, maybe I was a flesh-eating demoness too in some past life.'

'It's what I aspire to be in my next,' Pia half-jokes, and Clara flashes her a smile.

'So, how's the boyfriend doing? Is he behaving himself now?'

'I don't care anymore,' Pia says, shrugging.

'You know what, I oddly believe you,' Clara replies, and then wiggles her eyebrows. 'Who's the other guy, then?'

Pia looks at her with a confused expression, startled by her clairvoyance.

'Come on, Pia. I know that face. That is the face of someone who is getting it on the regular. You looked starved the last time I saw you – I mean, for dick, not food, *obviously*. And now, I suspect, it's the other way around.'

'I don't kiss and tell, Clara,' Pia says, flashing her a very telltale smile.

'So, you're not gonna let go of Raghav after all then? I take it the other guy's not loaded – in the other department, I mean,' she says with a wink.

'Yes. And I'm a hypocrite,' Pia says, her voice suddenly turning small and miserable.

'Hey, we all made some kind of deal with the devil to get here,' Clara shrugs.

I like this one – the demon chimes in at this point. *She gets us, no?*

'Plus,' Clara's saying now, as she sucks thoughtfully on her cigarette – 'Broke dick really is the best dick!'

Pia tries hard to keep a straight face, but fails to, dissolving into giggles. Meanwhile, Clara's laughing so hard, she needs to grab Pia's hand for support.

'Wow,' she hears a male voice say. They turn around to see Kabir standing right behind them, in a formal white shirt paired with denims, a bouquet of flowers in his hand.

'Oh, fuck,' Pia whispers.

He flings the bouquet at her feet, before exiting from the back gate.

'Kabir, wait!' Pia yells, running after him, which only makes him increase his pace.

They're out on the street now. Pia's breathless, her feet hurt and blistered from the strappy heels digging into them.

'She was joking, Kabir.'

'I'm sorry, but is that what I am to you? A *joke*?' he says, turning around.

She's never seen him this mad before.

He's never yelled this loud, and there's a vein on his forehead that looks about to burst.

'Kabir, no. I am sorry,' she whispers, tearing up.

He shakes his head, saying through gritted teeth, 'No, you're not. Pia, look at yourself, for fuck's sake. You're one of them now.'

'Kabir, don't go, *please*. I love you,' she yells at him. She realizes she really means it.

He looks like he doesn't know whether to laugh or punch a wall.

'No, you don't.'

'I do,' she pleads through her tears. 'I was … going to end it with Raghav. Please, Kabir.'

He continues shaking his head, now running a hand through his hair in frustration. Then he shrugs, 'I am sorry, but I can't, Pia. I don't even recognize you anymore. Whatever you have become – it disgusts me. You disgust me.'

He starts walking away, and she's in half a mind to chase him, but then the voice speaks up: *It's fine. Let him go. Clara was right. He's a broke hippie. He's no use to you, or me.*

'Not now,' Pia whispers, her sniffles turning into sobs, as she makes her way back to the main gallery.

She still can't go inside and finds herself sinking into the steps outside the back exit door, and going through the cigarettes in her pack like they're candy.

Clara finds her again.

'You gotta stop punishing yourself, babe,' she says to her, looking down at Pia, who is hunched into a ball on the steps.

Craning her neck to look up at Clara, her eyes filled with tears, Pia says, 'I fucked up.'

'No, you didn't. Trust me, I've been down this road before, and it's never ended well. It wouldn't have worked out with that guy anyway. I am sure whatever you had was great, but it wasn't real. You belong to different worlds.'

'Yeah, well, I hate this world,' Pia says, wiping her nose with the back of her hand. 'I thought I was better than all of this. But I am not. I am just like the rest of the sick people in this room.'

'So what are you gonna do? Leave it all behind to protest on the streets or live in an ashram in the Himalayas with him? Get real, Pia. And this – right here – *is* the real world, which you fit into as perfectly as you do in size-zero dresses, by the way,' she says, adding, 'You're one of them now, and tonight, you really do own this bloody place. Just admit it and *embrace* it.'

'You're right,' Pia sighs.

Clara raises the bottle of beer in her hand in a drunken toast: 'To Pia! Welcome to the real world, and best of luck. Lord knows you'll need it.'

She hands the bottle to Pia, who takes a big swig.

'Umm … excuse me? Do you have a light?' a shrill voice says from behind.

Pia turns around to find Sonia standing there.

Oh, she picked the wrong night to show her face, Pia's thinking now.

She looks as good in real life, as she does in her filtered social media pictures. So young, so tiny … in her virginal white, Greek toga-style dress. So clueless about who she is standing in front of, for the first ten seconds at least. Pia enjoys watching the moment the recognition slowly starts dawning on Sonia's face, making her friendly smile droop a little, even as her feet take a few hurried steps back.

'I am sorry, I just … I need to head back in there,' she says, backing away faster now, though not fast enough.

Pia closes the gap between them.

'Oh my God, you're Sonia, right?' she says, mock-chirpily. 'I'm a big fan of your YouTube channel and your Insta page, girl!'

She turns to look at Clara, who looks confused for a second, before finally registering the new arrival's name. 'Oh, me too!' she chimes in, giving an equally over-the-top performance.

'Your yoga moves!' Pia says, looking at her with utmost devotion now.

'So bendy!' Clara ad-libs.

'Right?' Pia exclaims at her friend, before turning to Sonia and giving her a dangerous smile, 'Raghav must love that … you know, in *bed*?'

Clara gives her a shocked look, but Pia can't stop. 'You know, Raghav? My boyfriend? The one you're *fucking*?'

Before Sonia can reply, Pia's already moved on to, 'Love your dress, by the way. Is that synthetic?'

'Yeah. Listen … I am sorry, but I really need to go …' The poor thing looks like she's about to break into a run.

'Where are you going? You wanted a light, *no*?' Pia says to her, as Clara hands her a zippo. 'Here, take it.'

'No, I really need to … to … to get inside,' Sonia's stammering now.

'That's okay. Take it. I insist,' Pia responds, except, instead of handing her the zippo, she clicks it open, aiming the flame at Sonia's crotch and watching the flimsy material of her dress light up.

'Pia! That was so *bad*!' she hears Clara chuckle, over Sonia's cries of pure terror.

Pia stands there, watching the edges of Sonia's dress being licked by the flames, laughing gleefully as well.

Sonia is now whirling like a dervish and screaming at the top of her lungs.

Suddenly, a familiar voice jolts her out of her trance.

'Pia! What the hell are you doing?' her mother is screaming, as she bursts out the back door.

'It was Clara,' Pia looks around, but her friend's missing. 'I mean, she egged me on, mom,' she shrugs, wondering if she's really losing her mind, after all.

'What are you talking about, Pia? Clara is inside. I've been speaking to her for the last fifteen minutes,' her mother says. *So, what are you gonna do? Leave it all behind to live in a Himalaya ashram with him?* Pia finally recognizes the suspiciously familiar words.

The demon is laughing even harder now, as she says, *Mmm, nothing like the taste of blood, and the sounds of terrified human screams.*

Neeta

She knew something was wrong, the moment she had set her eyes on Pia's paintings.

She couldn't understand how people were so entranced by the works of a clearly disturbed mind. The paintings were absolutely gruesome and grotesque, spelling out clearly that Pia was seriously, seriously sick.

The women in it, their features getting blurrier and uglier, with each progressive canvas, looked like they were baying for blood. Pia had always had a sick obsession with monsters, courtesy of Ila, but her technique had always been impeccable. These bleeding colours, blurry features, haphazard limbs ... they were all *a cry for help.*

As was her behaviour at Khushi's party, and her not calling or responding to Neeta's messages in the days that followed.

Neeta looked around the room to see if anyone else could see it. But they were all too busy, talking, laughing, drinking wine, and eating cheese and crackers. No one could see her baby was falling apart.

How could they all not see it?

As she looks at Pia's eyes now – recalling her laughter while she watched that poor girl burn – Neeta knows it is too late.

Those eyes.

Yellow and filled with venom.

Neeta has seen them like that before, and she knows what it means.

The demon's back.

12

JUNE 2004

Pia

She stares into the mirror of the bathroom of St Vincent's Girls Convent School. Her plump face is flush with a new outbreak of acne, while her curly hair has been pulled back in a tight braid. She's afraid her mom might soon notice that her green pinafore is too tight again. She bends down to splash some water on her face, and on turning around, she doesn't expect to see Ila, a classmate she's never spoken to before, but considers the coolest, most beautiful girl she's ever seen in her life, standing right behind her.

Her hair is short, pixie-cut, that accentuates her beautiful, delicate features – round eyes, framed by never-ending eyelashes, with a button nose and full, rosebud lips. They're even rose coloured, which Pia suspects is courtesy lipstick that's clearly against the school's rules.

So is folding the sleeves of one's shirt.

As is the bottle of spray paint she's holding in one of her hands.

She grins mischievously at Pia's reflection in the mirror, as she says, 'Run away, Miss goody two-shoes. You don't want to be here when they find out.'

Without waiting to watch her leave, Ila turns around to focus on the stalls, and starts spraying a weird-looking symbol on each of their doors.

Pia continues to stand there transfixed, shocked by the girl's brazenness, as she goes about patiently spraying large circles on the doors, with a star inside each.

When she turns around, Ila isn't mad to find Pia still there. Instead, she whispers conspiratorially to her, 'It's the anti-Christ symbol. Sister Stella's gonna be so mad!'

She claps her hands in glee, after throwing the bottle of paint through the window.

'You're not going to rat on me, are you?' she says to Pia, who shakes her head vigorously.

'Good, good. Because the bitch deserves it. She confiscated my Mills and Boons last week. Said I better be careful with books like these, because "Jesus is always watching me, all the time". Isn't that weird and freaky? So, I have decided, since I am being constantly watched, I might as well put on a good show.'

Just then, they hear the rustle of Sister Stella's cream sari, as she walks in. Despite being only 4'9'', she has the intimidating and terrifying presence of someone much taller that makes Pia suddenly develop the urge to empty out her bowels, or throw up her tiffin. However, Ila looks absolutely unaffected.

The nun's eyes wander past the guilty-looking Pia, and the unruffled girl next to her, to the bathroom stalls. She gasps.

'Who did this?'

'I don't know … I d-d-d-didn't see …' Pia begins.

'Actually, I saw some girl running down the corridor five minutes back. It still looks fresh to me, so I am guessing it might be her?' Ila says calmly.

'Well, how convenient for you, Ila.'

'Hey, I didn't do this!'

Sister Stella walks over to them, and grabs the girl's ear, wringing it tightly. 'I know you did it,' she says fiercely, and then turns to Pia, 'She did it, didn't she?'

Pia stammers again – 'I d-d-d-didn't see. I swear, Sister!'

Ila sounds irritated and impatient, when she says, 'Why don't you believe me? Look, there's no paint or spray bottle here with me. I saw the girl running away with one, maybe you could catch her if you move fast.'

'I am not going to chase after some imaginary girl for your entertainment, Ila. You come to the principal's office with me right now!' Sister Stella says, grabbing Ila's hand and hauling her out of the bathroom.

'And you!' she turns to look around at Pia, who is shaking at this point. 'Stop defending her, and for God's sake, stay away from her! This girl is the devil itself.'

As proof, Ila flashes her the most evil smile, and winks before she's dragged away from the loo.

Pia knows, in that moment, that she's finally found a friend.

In the coming months, she and Ila become inseparable. Pia can't get enough of just looking at her, or hearing the words coming out of her mouth, or following her around like her little, lost lamb.

She finds herself hacking off her hair to imitate Ila's, rolling her Rs just like Ila does, downloading the entire Red Hot Chili

Peppers playlist because that's what Ila listens to, and covering up the walls of her bedroom in posters that are the exact replica of the ones she's seen in Ila's.

Which suits Ila just fine, as she thrives on Pia's devotion. An aspiring Wiccan and tantric, she's glad she finally has a subject to deliver her hours-long sermons to.

Pia's fascinated with all the random information Ila keeps spouting – about succubi, huldras, Lilith, Japanese snow demons and Carribean Diablesse. She likes to drag Pia to the neighbouring jungles and leave little stick figurines and sage for the appeasement of whatever spirits she believes reside there.

The first time she brings Ila home, her friend can't stop cursing.

'Stop it, mom will hear you,' Pia shushes her.

'But this fucking house, Pia! It's like a castle. How many rooms are there, really? Do you even know? I bet you have a secret cellar, or some demons haunting a couple of the rooms.'

'You need to stop with the demons.'

'And you need to embrace their powers.'

They walk past the main verandah to the swimming pool on the other end of the property.

'Of course, you have a fucking swimming pool. Okay, we'll be chilling here all day,' she says, before being distracted by a small room by the deck. 'Are those the same chairs as Joey's and Chandler's in Friends*?' she screams excitedly.*

After that, Ila has become a permanent fixture in their household. Something her mother doesn't exactly approve of.

'I don't want you to hang out with that girl too much,' she tells Pia.

'Why?'

'I just don't … like her. She seems fast.*'*

'What makes you think she's fast?'

'She's already so … developed.'

'How is that her fault, mom? That's biology.'

'Well, then she doesn't have to stick out her butt and boobs like that. Attracting the wrong kind of attention all the time.'

'Gross, mom,' Pia shakes her head.

In the days that follow, she clings to Ila even tighter.

Her mother doesn't even realize how much her life has changed since Ila entered it.

Her mother doesn't know she'll do anything for Ila.

A few weeks later, they're spending the day in the swimming pool again. Ila's sprawled on a float, with a glass of orange juice in one hand and some book on demons in the other.

Pia feels both envy and admiration at the sight of her friend in a floral string bikini. Pia – on the other hand – dived in, wearing her shorts and tee, because the thought of herself venturing into broad daylight in nothing but a swimming costume is way more terrifying to her than any of Ila's demons.

'I wish you'd just let go of your body hang-ups,' she's telling Pia now.

'And I wish I were as skinny as you.'

'Will you sell your soul to the demon to get that?'

'Of course. It can take it. I don't want it anyway.'

'Well, that's stupid. You just need to stop hiding underneath all that baggy stuff!'

She sounds like Pia's mom, when she talks like this. Neeta's constantly telling Pia to stop hiding her face, sorry 'their' face, even making Pia grow out her bangs because they seemed to block her line of vision.

Ila has moved on to her book now. 'It says here that in India, the closest we have to demons are the yakshinis. There are both benevolent and malevolent ones. They are described as having round feminine hips and big bosoms.'

'Great, even demons have to succumb to society's unrealistic body standards,' Pia groans.

'Of course, they do, dummy. To seduce men ... and, wow, drink their blood afterwards.'

'Yuck.'

'It also says here that they grant wishes,' says Ila.

'You know I was joking when I said I'd sell my soul to get skinny, right?' Pia replies, but Ila is no longer listening.

'It's final. We are summoning a demon this Friday.'

Pia isn't sure if Ila is doing this to terrify her for kicks – because she often does that – or if she actually wants to meet a yakshini ('We'll call a benevolent one, don't worry,' she'd told Pia).

All she knows is that this is a terrible idea.

Still in their school uniforms, they're seated in Pia's garden, a fire burning in front of them. Ila stares at it intently, as she chants unintelligible mantras, over and over.

It's getting late, the sun is almost down, and there are quite a few mosquitoes buzzing around. Pia wants to stop, but she knows it is not an option.

She's worried someone will find them, even though they've specifically chosen a Friday evening, because it's the day her mum's kitty gang assembles at the club, and Khushi has her guitar practice, and with no one home, the domestic staff make themselves scarce as well.

No one will find them here for hours.

Ila is still repeating the same mantras, and they're giving Pia a headache now. She swats miserably at the mosquitoes, bored out of her mind.

And then she hears a loud bang.

The sky goes completely black, and the fire blows out. Pia turns around to look at the house behind them, but it looks like there's a blackout in there as well.

There's a deathly silence, before a loud, deep, rumbling laughter disrupts it.

Pia squints through the darkness, to see if Ila is the one laughing, though she's heard her friend laugh and it's nowhere near as loud or strange.

This laughter … it doesn't even sound human.

'If this is a prank, Ila … if you're playing a tape recorder or something, I swear I will fucking kill you,' she warns Ila, who replies through the darkness, 'What do you mean? Do you hear something?'

'The laughter – how do you not hear it, Ila? It's so loud!'

'Wait, are you trying to play a prank on ME? Because you're doing a good job, and I would like you to stop now,' Ila is saying.

That's when Pia realizes, the voice is inside her.

Ila can't hear it.

'Ila, something strange is happening to me,' she whispers now, confused and afraid.

'Pia, stop it!'

'She's talking to me,' Pia whispers.

Tears start to stream down her face. This, she realizes, is real. This is really happening. No human could speak in a voice like this. It's deep and feminine, but certainly not a woman's.

It sounds more like an ancient creature's, one that's learnt to speak like humans, which makes it absolutely terrifying.

'She's inside me, Ila,' she sobs to her friend now. 'She says her name is Bhishna.'

'Fuck,' Ila says. 'Pia, if you are joking, now is the time to stop.'

'Is she …' Pia is so afraid, she can barely speak – 'Is she one of the bad ones?'

Ila doesn't respond.

'Why aren't you replying, Ila?'

Because she's heard my name before, *the voice rumbles inside Pia.*

'She's malevolent, Pia,' Ila finally says, followed by a 'I am so, so sorry.'

Pia can hear her crying too.

That's harsh. You know, some people pray to me as well. I am quite revered in some parts.

And quite full of yourself too, Pia can't help but think to herself.

Ah, you're feisty, aren't you? *says the demon now.*

The very last thing Pia would ever describe herself as is 'feisty'.

Oh, but you are, you just don't know it. You're a lost, little thing. That makes you even more special to me. My whole purpose is guiding lost souls like yours, *she's saying now.*

Somewhere far away, Ila is shouting words she can barely hear, 'Pia, are you okay?'

'No, I am not, Ila. There's a demon inside me,' Pia snaps at her.

'I am so sorry,' Ila continues saying, over and over.

'Fat load of good your sorries will do for me now, Ila,' Pia screams.

'What is she saying to you?' Ila asks her.

'She's saying that I have to kill Tuffy,' Pia tells her friend.

Tell her that I can see into the future, *the voice in her belly eggs her on.* That in his next life, Tuffy will be reincarnated as a horse.

But when Pia says it out loud, the ridiculousness of the statements gets Ila's tears to dry up. She bursts out laughing instead.

'Come on, you really expect me to believe the demon's saying this bullshit. Stop now, the joke's over.'

'No, I'm serious. She's saying he has better things in store for him,' Pia shouts at her friend in frustration.

Right on cue, they hear Tuffy, Pia's pet labrador, approaching them.

'You're going to kill Tuffy!' Ila's laughing so hard now, she can't breathe. 'And then he'll become a horse. Pia, what the fuck? You suck at practical jokes.'

'I believe her,' Pia continues to argue.

Ila doesn't stop laughing until Tuffy's moans and whimpers pierce the air. When the lights come on two minutes later, her eyes travel from the piece of blood-covered wood in Pia's hands to the dog's dead body lying on the floor, and then to both their pinafores that are soaked in blood.

'You fucking stabbed Tuffy?'

'She asked me to. I told you she asked me to,' Pia tells her friend.

Ila lets out a huge chilling scream, and suddenly Pia's mom arrives.

'What is happening?' Neeta says, as she takes in the scene in front of her.

'Pia, what have you done?' she screams.

'She asked me to, mom.'

'I didn't ask her to do anything, aunty. She's fucking crazy,' Ila shrieks.

'Not you,' Pia tries to clarify. 'The Yakshini, she asked me to. Ila, tell her. Tell my mom about the demon,' she pleads to her friend, throwing the piece of wood away, as she runs to her.

'Get away from me, you freak!' Ila yells, backing away like she can't get far enough from Pia.

Pia feels her mother yank her arm, trying to drag her away from the scene. But just as she's about to leave, Ila lets out another scream.

'Pia, your eyes!'

'What?' Pia looks at her friend, confused.

'They're fucking yellow!'

13

Pia

She stares at the bodies lying on the pavement in a forgotten heap, fast asleep at 3 a.m. Next to her, the phone buzzes relentlessly.

She stays there, staring at them, until one of them wanders dazedly to the middle of the street.

He's clearly in the way, the demon is saying now.

Don't worry, no one will miss him, Pia, it urges her.

She changes gears, and slams her feet on the accelerator, revelling in the sounds of his knees crumpling against the bumper, and the loud smashing of the glass, as his head hits the windscreen.

When she checks her phone, ten minutes later, she has three voicemails.

She clicks on the one from Kabir – 'Pia, I love you too … but you have to sort your head out. You have to decide what you want. I can't take anymore of it, and I know you're better than this. You're a good person; don't let them take this away from you.'

Next, her mother's voice fills the air – 'Pia beta, come

back. I know it's back, and we can get rid of it. This is my mistake. I should have never let you out of my sight. I shouldn't have left you alone. I love you, beta, just come back, and we'll make this all go away.'

And finally, a drunk Raghav slurs – 'Pia, I am so fucking proud of you. This place is blowing up. They can't stop talking about the brilliant artist that you are. And you deserve it, baby. All of it. You know what, I just had this *insane* idea – let's get married. Tonight, or well, maybe tomorrow, since the courts will be shut right now. I just don't want to wait anymore.'

She bursts into laughter, and continues laughing for fifteen minutes, until her stomach hurts.

Until that laughter starts to slowly transform into strangled sobs.

14

Neeta

Pia shows up at their front gate at 4 a.m., looking like a ghost of herself. Her hair is wild and tangled, her cheeks hollowed out and her eyes a sleepless red.

She smells awful too, Neeta realizes once she's closer.

Her out-of-control mane, dark circles and rancid body odour contrast and clash jarringly with the short, red dress she's wearing that's tight enough to reveal she's lost too much weight.

Her body looks skeletal, Neeta notices with alarm, and so does her face, with her features stretched out grotesquely across what's remaining of it.

Suddenly, Pia grabs her head, and lets out a long, tortured cry. To Neeta, in that moment, she looks exactly like the distorted woman from Edvard Munch's haunting piece, 'Scream'.

'She's back, mom. She's back!' her daughter yells over and over.

'I know ...' Neeta says, hugging her tightly, in an attempt to calm her down. It hurts to hold her now. Her sharp, protruding bones poke Neeta in the arms and chest.

The narrow streets outside their bungalow are practically deserted at this hour, but it won't be long before the first of the geriatric uncles ventures out for a walk. Through the corner of her eye, she can see the lights in the neighbouring kothis switch on. Their guards step out of their cubicles besides the gates, and walk up closer to the Bhandari bungalow, to take in this spectacle.

'Let's not create a scene here outside, beta,' she starts ushering Pia in, before the neighbours can see.

In reply, Pia lets out another bloodcurdling scream. Her feet remain rooted to the ground as she flings Neeta off her, refusing to budge from her spot, looking around her frantically.

'Make it shut up, mom. Please!' she pleads.

Neeta spots Ajit running towards the gate now, in his kurta-pyjamas and panic mode, carrying a cricket bat in his hand. 'What happened, beta? Are you okay?' he looks stricken at the sight of his daughter.

'IT WON'T STOP TALKING TO ME!' Pia keeps screaming through her sobs, her hands now tearing at her hair. 'Make her go away, dad!' she begs.

Ajit looks helpless in return, and Neeta can empathize with him in that moment. He has never seen his daughter like this before – and she senses the terror gripping him. He doesn't seem to understand what is happening. His brain – which was seeking an external intruder to swing his bat at – is clearly short-circuiting. As a result, he continues to clutch the bat, in a position that's a cross between a half-batting squat and half-attack mode. His eyes wander from Pia's face to the surrounding vicinity, looking for some sort of an explanation. Neeta finds her empathy turning into annoyance.

'What are you doing?' she snaps at him. 'Let's take her inside!'

'Yes, you're right,' he says, still looking around, as though hoping to catch the bastard who did this to his daughter.

Meanwhile, Pia is screaming her head off, setting off a car alarm or two in the process.

Then, Ajit finally seems to spot something. 'Wait,' he says, approaching Pia's yellow Volkswagen Beetle slowly.

Neeta follows him. When she's six steps away from the car, she sees it. The windshield of the car is cracked and caved in – with a hole in it the size of a human head. And smeared across it, as well as the bonnet, and the number plate, is blood.

She turns around to look at Pia, who is still standing in the same spot.

'It told me to kill him,' her daughter is saying now. 'It won't stop telling me to do things.'

Ajit is now completely lost. 'What is she talking about, Neeta?' he asks his wife in a helpless voice.

She ignores him, still staring at Pia, as déjà vu sets in.

'Who did you run over, Pia?' she asks her daughter.

'One of those men sleeping on the pavement outside,' Pia replies.

She did it on purpose, Neeta realizes, afraid. Next to her, Ajit comes to the same realization.

There's a long eerie silence, including from Pia, who

has finally stopped screaming and left the spot where she was standing. Now, she's hunched in the corner, besides the Beetle, like a feral animal, whimpering to herself.

Finally, Neeta breaks it, saying in a steady voice, 'She's out of her mind, Ajit. If this goes to court, an insanity plea has to hold up, right?'

15

Neeta

When she woke up again, Pia wouldn't stop screaming, which is why Dr Agarwal is here.

Neeta actually prefers her screaming version, because when Pia isn't screaming, she's talking and saying things she definitely doesn't want to hear.

Things like, 'He isn't the first one …'

'First what?' Neeta asks her, despite herself.

'Person that I have killed,' Pia's eyes are dead now, her daughter gone from them. What remains is this strange, outer skeletal shell of Pia. 'There have been others,' she continues. 'I killed one last month as well. Why do you think I look like this?' – Pia says, gesturing to her face and body, as they all stand around her in the living room.

'What?' says Ajit, who has aged a decade in the last hour, and seems to be increasingly questioning his own sanity.

'The demon, dad,' Pia explains to him, enunciating each word slowly as though explaining to a five-year-old.

'It gives me whatever I want – as long as I do what she says.'

'So, this demon … it … told you to hit the guy with your car?' Ajit asks her, followed by, 'And what about the other person you are saying you killed? Who was he? What happened to him?'

'A labourer at a building under construction. I pushed him. Don't worry, I made it look like an accident. Besides, no one will notice he's gone, dad,' Pia tells him.

It is surreal, watching her own daughter, so fragile-looking in that beautiful dress, confess to murders she's committed or *think*s she's committed.

Neeta still isn't sure she believes it all.

She doesn't know why, seeing as how, unlike Ajit, she has seen this side of Pia before. The side that's capable of anything.

'Do you believe her?' Neeta asks Ajit and Dr Agarwal, once Pia has been sedated.

'That's for the police to investigate …' Ajit interjects.

'She can't have done it … she's a *child*. And she's sick.'

Dr Agarwal shakes his head at her, saying, 'She is almost thirty, and what you are experiencing right now is a type of cognitive dissonance. The truth is, Pia is more than capable of doing this. It isn't surprising at all, Neeta. She exhibited signs of this much earlier on in life.'

'Neeta, what is he talking about?' Ajit asks her incredulously.

'Not right now, Ajit,' Neeta shushes him, infuriated that Dr Agarwal would pick this moment to finally realize what she had been warning him about all along. She had warned him, hadn't she? And all he had done in exchange was prescribe her sleeping pills.

'You've been postponing this conversation for twenty years now. I think it's time I put my foot down,' Ajit is saying to her now.

Neeta has no choice but to tell him about everything.

'Why didn't you tell me this before?' Ajit asks Neeta, when she's done.

'I was afraid … for her, for myself. I felt that I could solve the problem. Instead I ended up feeding the beast, didn't I?' Neeta whispers, teary-eyed.

'I don't know, Neeta. And what's worse is that I don't know how to fix this … at this point.'

Then they hear their daughter's voice from the other side of the room, quiet and groggy, 'Don't worry, dad. I'll fix it.'

Pia

They are not listening to her. Or perhaps they heard her and are deliberately ignoring her.

'I'll fix it!' she yells now, and they look towards her. Dr Agarwal seems amazed that she's still talking after that giant dose of sedatives he gave her.

It's too less, too late, doc. You're gonna have to give me something much, much stronger this time. Maybe that stuff they use to tranquilize horses? The demon cackles inside her head.

Pia ignores it, saying again, 'I can fix this. I can make it all go away. I mean, the demon can.'

Oh, now you want me to play fairy godmother again? After screaming and bitching about me to your family for the past hour? Fuck you, Pia.

'Is this demon talking to you right now, beta?' her mother asks her kindly.

'Yes, she is,' Pia replies.

'See? She is completely delusional,' her mother tells the other two immediately after, as though resting her case.

Pia feels oddly betrayed, but she doesn't have the time to feel hurt. She has to convince them she isn't crazy. That she's got a handle on this whole situation.

'I am not delusional,' she yells, racking her brains to find evidence to prove it.

'Wait!' she says. 'Listen to this—'

Pia holds up her cellphone.

And despite themselves, the three other people in the room lean in, in anticipation.

Soon, Raghav's deep, desperate voice fills the air –

'Pia, I am so fucking proud of you. This place is blowing up. They can't stop talking about the brilliant artist that you are. And you deserve it, baby. All of it. You know what, I just had this insane *idea – let's get married. Tonight, or well, maybe tomorrow, since the courts will be shut right now. I just don't want to wait anymore.'*

Pia smiles brightly once Raghav's done talking.

'See?' she says, waving her cellphone at them.

They all lean back, their expressions an amalgamation of disappointment, pity, concern and *fear.*

Now, they look like they are *convinced* that she is insane.

... *Because they don't get it.*

'The demon,' she says, excitedly. 'It gives me whatever I want, in return for doing what it wants me to, remember? It wanted me to run over that guy back there, in exchange for Raghav proposing ... It's all quid pro quo. Like, a ... a human sacrifice! Don't you see? That's how I'll make all of this go away!'

Her mother's talking over her now – 'Maybe Pia's right ... maybe no one will notice.'

'About that ...' Pia interrupts her. 'The body might still be there.'

'And it will all be captured on the CCTV,' Ajit adds.

'But you can make it all go away, can't you, Ajit?' Neeta pleads.

'How many people are we supposed to be paying off here – the victim, the victim's family, the eye-witnesses, the police? And *should* we be? Just look at her right now. She is clearly dangerous,' her dad is arguing.

'So what do we do then? Send her to jail?' her mother yells.

'That's where she belongs, Neeta,' her dad sighs, wiping his face wearily with his hand.

'She's your daughter. And she isn't well! You can see that. You can make this go away. All of it. You know you can, Ajit!'

'Well, yes, but she's a danger to everyone around her, to *us* ...'

'You're being really unfair.'

'I'm a judge, Neeta. Being fair is my job.'

'That's the problem, Ajit. I don't need you to be a judge right now. I need you to think like a father.'

'I can fix this,' Pia pleads again from her corner.

Are you sure? Because after that stunt you pulled, I want something more, something bigger – the demon is saying.

'It'll make it go away,' Pia continues whimpering, but the three ignore her. 'But it wants something in return.'

No reaction. They're all still a little too busy discussing her in third person, while she's standing right there.

Tell them. Tell them what I want.

'SHE WANTS ONE OF YOU,' Pia finally roars in a voice unlike hers. The room falls quiet, as they all fix their eyes on her.

They are staring at her as though she's a rabid animal or a ticking bomb. She feels like a bit of both.

'Which one …' her father's voice cracks as he says this. He tries again, in a careful, measured tone this time, 'Which one of us does it want?'

The doc. I want the fucking doc. That fat bastard deserves what's coming for him anyway.

Pia turns her gaze to the doctor. He looks nervous, his face suddenly slick with sweat. His Adam's apple bobbing around madly.

Him, she says, but the voice isn't hers.

In fact, her body doesn't feel in her control either; the demon has taken over the wheel. She doesn't have to do anything. It's an entity of its own.

Flinging itself across the room, it grabs a lamp, and brings it crashing down on Dr Agarwal's skull. But she doesn't hear the *thwack* of the paperweight against his skull.

It doesn't matter.

Because now her hand is being grabbed and twisted, and she's landing on the floor. Her mother lets out loud, deafening shrieks, as Pia feels her own skull go – not *thwack*, not *thud* – but *splat* against the floor.

She blacks out instantly.

16

TWO MONTHS LATER

Pia

She wakes up in a room, feeling completely disoriented and panicking at the sight of her unfamiliar surroundings. It's all too much – visually (the room with stark white walls, a small window, a bed, a steel table besides it) and sensorily (the rough blanket and papery nightgown scratching against her skin, the freezing air-conditioning, the smell of antiseptic). Then, she remembers. It's just the psychiatric institution, called Aastha, Sadhana or something like that, somewhere on the outskirts of Delhi. Pia was too zoned out to keep track of where they were going exactly.

She's only been here a day. She was transferred directly from the hospital – where she was being treated for her skull fracture. She remembers the different tubes inserted into her arms and nose, and she can see the scars from where they broke her skin, but she doesn't feel a thing. She tries sitting up, but her body no longer complies to her broken, drugged-up brain. Finally, after some struggle, and animal-like sounds, she's upright, before the world spins off its axis.

Just as Pia's about to try standing up, the door opens, and a woman dressed in green scrubs walks in. Her name tag reads: Savita.

'Easy, Pia. Don't try standing up without assistance, yet. You'll fall,' Savita's saying to her in a bright, high-pitched voice. She's carrying a tray, comprising an omelette and two toasts, orange juice, an apple and a cute, deceptive little cup with, Pia suspects, a lethal dosage of medicines. Pia wolfs it all down, as Savita reads out the day's schedule to her – a session with Dr Sengupta, yoga, lunch, free time, an art therapy class, bedtime.

'I am so glad you're eating again,' Savita says, with a smile. 'And welcome to *Prarthana*!'

Right. Prarthana.

Pia suddenly feels claustrophobic, and an urge to knock Savita out of her way, before running away.

But when she shuffles out of the room, her great escape plan is thwarted by the realization that her pace is now slower than a turtle's and she has to lean pathetically on Savita the whole time.

They escort her to the bathroom, and she takes in her surroundings along the way. It's much like any other hospital, in that it is a series of long white corridors, dotted with different rooms housing patients and doctor's offices. Patients dressed like her in grey gowns, as well as in casuals, are wandering sedately – or in some cases, skidding gleefully – down the hallway, or peeking out at her from the holes in their doors.

'We also have a yoga room, and a dance room, and of course, an art therapy space, which I am sure you will love,' Savita chirps on, as though reading Pia's mind. 'There's a garden outside. Maybe you can see it in a day or two.'

When they reach their destination – a large, blue-tiled bathroom, divided into showering and toilet cubicles – Savita helps her strip for a bath.

Though there are no mirrors around, Pia only has to look down to see that all the weight she had lost has found its way back to her. Her stomach is now vast and doughy, her legs look flabbier than ever. She thinks tenderly about her thigh gap for a moment, before squeezing her eyes shut to hold back the tears. The urge to run is back, but she doesn't think her naked, soaped-up and sedated body will carry her past the door of this bathroom, let alone the gates of this mental institution.

And so she submits to Savita's vigorous, almost violent, scrubbing process, and her fate.

Pia doesn't know if she can make it through this therapy session. She feels too slow and stupid to form coherent thoughts and then translate them into speech. In fact, she can barely sit up and feels herself gently glide down the yellow sofa, until she's half-lying on it, with her knees splayed out in front of her.

Thankfully, Dr Sengupta doesn't react in any way to her ungraceful posture.

The first thing Pia notices is how different he looks from Dr Agarwal. Not that she thought all psychiatrists look the same, but she'd always pegged them to be over forty-five at the least. This guy looks like he must barely be out of shrink school. He's even dressed in jeans and a grey hoodie. She squints a little and realizes that he might even be quite attractive for a psychiatrist – even though his hair is a little too curly, his nose stubby and his eyes so tiny they almost disappear when he smiles.

'Dr Sengupta …' she begins.

'Call me Anando,' he says, scribbling into his notepad. His office is a cozy space, a far cry from Dr Agarwal's. The walls are lemon yellow, with colourful charts plastered all over. A big framed sign on one of them reads:

> *'It is no measure of health to be well adjusted to a profoundly sick society.'*
>
> – J. Krishnamurti

The sofa she's sitting on is a pretty shade of blue. The whole setup, Pia feels, has a warm, paediatric vibe to it, while Anando looks like the kind of doctor who'll give you candy if you don't cry during injections.

'Anando,' she begins again, with some effort. 'I don't think I can do this today …'

She notices her speech is slurred. He does, too. It makes him scribble something more, before putting down his pen and smiling at her, 'We don't need to do *anything*, today,' he assures her, adding, 'I just wanted to drop by, say hello. Maybe ask you a few simple questions, if you're up for it.'

Pia nods her head with great effort.

'How do you feel?'

'I have no idea, I just woke up,' Pia says slowly to him. 'Just numb, I guess.'

'Yes, you're on quite a bit of medication, considering the state we found you in.'

He asks her a few simple questions: the date ('I don't know, I just woke up'), time (11 a.m.?), place ('mental hospital').

And then others that seem harder: Who's the president? ('my general knowledge sucks, doc. Can I tell you who the PM is instead?'), Can you spell this word, forwards and backwards? ('I don't know. Holding the pen sucks, too'), and a mathematical test ('I'm worse with numbers than I am with names of presidents').

He asks her to touch her nose with her right hand, which she does with some difficulty, throws a bunch of riddles at her, and finally calls it a day.

She looks for signs of how she did on his face, but finds nothing there. Instead, he tells her there'll be medical tests next, when she's up for it, and that Savita will escort her to the laboratory.

Through it all, Pia finds herself growing fonder of him, despite herself. She likes how his voice is friendly, with a hint of playfulness to it, she likes his untidy mop of hair and kind eyes, and how he smiles with his whole face, in a way that makes Pia smile in return.

'So now that we're all introduced,' he continues. 'It's time we took you to your mother.'

'Wait, she's here?' Pia clutches the sofa in panic.

'Yes, in the visitor's room,' he replies, carefully studying her reaction. 'I thought you'd be happy to see her.'

'I am not sure how I feel,' she admits.

'It'll take a while for you to feel like yourself. Don't worry, that's completely fine. Take your time,' he tells her.

He gets up, and she realizes he isn't very tall (somewhere between 5'6" and 5'8"?), and walks over to Savita for a brief chat. She then comes over to help Pia, who grimaces at the thought of having to be vertical, as well as seeing her mother.

Neeta

Pia looks like her daughter again, albeit a bit slower and rounder. It takes her a while to reach their table in the canteen, which reminds her of the one at Pia's school. Just a counter in front selling patties, chips, Coke and samosas, with desks and chairs scattered across in front of it. It's practically empty right now.

It's strange to see Pia like this – back to herself, her face scrubbed of makeup. She appears to be heavily sedated. For a moment, Neeta can't help but feel a little overdressed herself in the setting, her blue silk sari and Chanel No. 5 perfume clashing with the surroundings filled with the smell of medicines and antiseptics. When her daughter is standing in front of her, in that dowdy grey hospital gown, Neeta experiences a surreal sense of two parallel universes colliding, as well as a sudden urge to snatch Pia and take her back to her own.

'How are you?' after a quick hug, she asks. It sounds and feels all wrong, too formal. But it's difficult to see Pia like this. 'I got you samosas. I know how much you love them.'

Pia stares at Neeta silently for five seconds, leaving the samosas untouched, before sighing.

'How long will I be here?' she mumbles. Neeta notices how Pia's words are spaced out and prolonged.

'I don't know,' she says apologetically. 'They said you have to be under supervision for some time.'

'But what about Raghav, mom? He was going to propose, you know,' Pia looks like she's on the verge of crying now, and Neeta feels like she's on the verge of crying, too.

'He'll be there when you get out,' she lies.

'Okay, just don't tell him that I am here,' Pia says, chewing her lower lip thoughtfully.

When Neeta doesn't reply, she continues, 'The guy I hit … you know, with my car.'

'The accident,' Neeta reprimands.

'Mom …'

'It's taken care of, don't mention it to anyone, ever again.'

Pia chews her lower lip harder.

'And the other guy?'

'We have no way of confirming – with your condition, your delusions. There's really no saying whether it happened or not …'

'Delusions?' Pia repeats the word. 'Really?'

Feeling both guilt and frustration building up inside her, Neeta switches to the offensive, 'Pia, I am trying to save you. Why don't you ever get that? Do you know how hard it was to get you here, instead of jail?'

Now it's Pia's turn to fall silent.

'Look, everything's fine. You don't need to worry about anything apart from getting better. Starting over. That's all you need to do now, beta – *heal.*'

'Where's dad?' Pia asks her suddenly. 'Does Khushi know?'

'It's hard for them to …' Neeta begins, but Pia waves her off.

'Sure, I mean. I can understand how it's so hard for *you guys*. It's the same shit all over again. I don't think, deep down, any of you actually give a fuck about me.'

Pia looks completely coherent now. She flashes Neeta a small sad smile, before she adds in a voice that's completely steady, her speech no longer slurred and her words perfectly enunciated, 'I am never going to leave this place, am I? And Raghav won't wait either. I am not stupid, mom. I know none of you want anything to do with me anymore. You're glad you're finally rid of me.'

'That isn't true,' Neeta whispers fiercely, gripping Pia's hand tight. 'All we want is for you to get better, and come home. Just take care of yourself and be good,' she adds.

'You believe me, don't you? You know the demon's real.'

Neeta looks into her eyes, beginning to shake her head.

'Bullshit, you've seen it,' Pia spits out furiously, trying to break free from her grip, but Neeta holds on tight. 'I know you have.'

'Pia …'

'There are more, mom,' her daughter is saying now,

her voice dropping to a barely audible whisper, as she leans close to Neeta.

'More of what?' Neeta asks her.

'People … that I have killed. Many, many more,' Pia whispers softly. 'I fucking deserve to be here.'

'Promise me, you won't talk about it to anyone,' Neeta says, squeezing her daughter's hand tight, noticing that it's gone limp again.

'Promise me, Pia! They'll send you to jail this time if you do!' she says, gripping the hand tighter, shaking it to get her to pay attention. It flops around lifelessly.

The clarity is gone from Pia's eyes. She's somewhere far away now, and Neeta isn't sure if she can even hear her mother anymore.

17

Anando

A week after their first meeting, he goes through Pia's various test results, spread out on his table.

They tell him nothing. Apart from her abysmal general knowledge and even worse mathematical skills, there seems to be nothing technically wrong with her.

Her physical exam and lab test results rule out any hormonal, chemical, biological or drug-related imbalances.

And though her symptoms – depression, mania, delusions and hallucinations – correspond with a variety of disorders, his initial interactions with her provide him with very little clues regarding where to slot her on the spectrum.

'Just wanted to check in on how the new one was doing,' the director of the institute, Dr Khanna, says, inviting himself into Anando's office and plonking down on the sofa.

'Not sure. Her tests have been completely inconclusive.'

This piques his interest. 'She tried to kill her last psychiatrist and said the demon inside her head told her to do it. Not to mention, the anorexia … and you got *nothing*?'

Anando passes the tests over to him. 'She's depressed, of course, but other than that, I don't seem to have anything to go by. There's no demon in her head anymore, and she refuses to talk about it, or anything else, for that matter. But whenever she does talk, her thoughts sound balanced and coherent. So far, she's nothing like the girl in that file.'

'A split personality, perhaps?'

Anando shrugs. 'I am not ruling out anything. Though I think I'll try a more psychoanalytical approach next.'

'Oh, come on. It's either a dissociative identity disorder or schizophrenia. You don't have to bring Freud into this. Or waste more time than you need to.'

'I need her to open up to me, to talk freely, in order to figure out what's wrong,' Anando reasons with him.

It's always been a struggle to get through to the director, who believes in quantity over quality when it comes to patients and treatments. It's understandable, since they are understaffed and under-resourced. It's hard to give a patient the kind of attention required in circumstances such as these, and it gives you a special kind of distance from – and apathy towards – human suffering.

Dr Khanna himself seems to have that resigned look of someone who knows he'll live and die here, with the rest of the patients. In fact, he's begun to look a little crazy himself. He's huge – at least six feet tall and overweight, and what one would describe as hirsute. He certainly doesn't help matters by letting his beard, sideburns and ear hair grow unattended. Even his eyebrows are bushy. Sometimes it's hard to make out his expressions or what he's saying through all that hair. The only thing that sets him distinctly apart from everyone else here is his tailored suits.

Anando understands Dr Khanna's sense of dispassionateness, but it's hard for him to emulate it. He's too old-fashioned for that. He always likes to get overly involved, no matter how messy that may seem to the rest. He considers transference to be an inevitable – if not essential – part of therapy.

'Look, Anando, I know your tendency to *over-familiarize* yourself with patients in such cases, but it isn't worth it. This one's never leaving here, her family said as much to me.'

'Really?'

'Her father said she's dangerous, unpredictable, yada, yada, you know the usual story,' he says, with a dismissive wave. 'The most you can do in this situation is find her a combination of medicines – and a routine – that will keep her calm and under control. That's all this place asks of you. You don't need to do more.'

Anando doesn't tell the director that he is already over-involved. That his burning curiosity won't rest until he uncovers who that other Pia – the one in the file – is.

Where is she hiding? He wonders now.

What would make her come out?

Pia

She's back in her familiar black sweatshirt and jeans, which she feels is an odd comfort in this strange, new place.

Over the last few days, the numbness inside her head has given way to a heavy black depression, and frequent bouts of breathlessness, like her guilt is a giant rock crushing her chest.

She finds that in this state, she has little to say to Anando.

'We've got some new tests lined up today,' he's telling her now.

Pia shrugs. 'Shocking,' she replies with a sarcastic smile. *The guy's obsessed with tests.*

'We're going to try the Rorschach this time. You know about this one?' he says, holding a bunch of cards in his hand.

Pia nods. 'Mostly, from crime shows.'

'Yes, that's right. It's a bit controversial, and its results are not really accepted as formal diagnoses ...'

'Then, what's the point?' Pia asks him, as though she doesn't have all the time in the world to squander away on pointless tests.

'It might unlock something inside you, and it might help me understand what brought you here.'

Pia shrugs again. 'Suit yourself, doc.'

'Now, I'm going to hand you these one by one, and I want you to tell me what you see in them,' he says as he holds up the cards.

Pia realizes, from all her years of TV-watching experience, that sane, happy people see sane, happy things in these cards. The serial killers, on the other hand, see dismembered heads, and blood and penises and vaginas. It makes her nervous about what she might find in them.

He hands her the first one.

It's an ink blot shaped like a … vagina. Damn. Pia knows better than to say such a thing aloud. She squints at the vagina again, hoping to find something more acceptable in there, and finally notices it. 'A woman – an angel or demon – of some sort,' she replies, somehow knowing that wasn't the correct answer either.

He jots something down in his pad, and hands her the second one.

Great. More vaginas, thinks Pia, as she stares at the two black blobs, with two biggish red blobs on top, and two smaller red blobs at the bottom.

'It's a woman, with … bloody eyes …' she replies. *Wrong answer again. You should have just said vagina, you idiot. He* definitely *thinks you're a serial killer now.*

When she looks at the next card, she channels her whole being into finding something happy in it.

'Two men. Bowling?' she tells the doctor, who isn't looking at her, just scribbling notes in his pad. 'They look like they're having fun,' she adds, for extra brownie points.

However, her heart begins to thud loudly when she looks at the fourth card. *It's just a dumb card, with dumb ink blots on it,* she tries to reason with herself, but her heart continues to race at the image before her. A black imposing figure looking down at her, with demonic horns, and a thick long tail poking from beneath its legs. There is unspeakable violence in its stance, and Pia feels slow, chilling terror grip her frame.

'Pia, are you all right?' Anando is asking her from what feels like faraway, but when she looks up, he's right there, next to her, looking at her with a concerned expression. She takes a deep breath, and nods her head, pulling her sweatshirt sleeves down all the way past her hands, like she always does when nervous.

'It's a creature looking down at me. It looks like it's about to do something bad. To me,' she says, haltingly.

She's glad to see that Anando is still hiding his thoughts. She doesn't care what he thinks of her in the first place.

She isn't sure why but all the ink blots feel sinister to her right now. The bat she sees in the fifth card looks poised to attack her as well.

She doesn't mention that last part to Anando.

The sixth card looks even more like a vagina than the last two, but there's something unsettling about the dark black inky rendition of the female sex that resembles roadkill. Or perhaps it's her newfound phobia of ink blots that's messing with her head.

The same chilling terror returns with the seventh. In it, two identical old women stare at each other with extreme hostility. They look like witches to her, their hair flying in the air, standing in what's clearly a battle stance. She opens her mouth to explain this to Anando, but she can't speak. She realizes she's sweating.

They are just ink blots, Pia. she tells herself over and over, hoping Anando will say it's time to wrap things up.

But he remains silent, waiting for her response.

'Two old women, probably witches,' she says, no longer bothering to hide her derangement from him anymore.

The eighth card is a sudden burst of pink, blue, green and orange blots, which Pia dislikes. All she sees are two wild boars rising from the depths of hell, and tells Anando so. She sees a demon in the ninth, while the tenth appears to be the diseased insides of a person, complete with blood and parasites.

'I'm really sick, aren't I?' she asks him fearfully when she's finished.

'Relax, Pia. There's no right or wrong here,' he replies.

Anando

Well, he didn't exactly lie. There is certainly no objective right or wrong there. But, if he were to put it politely, Pia's responses were highly … *atypical.* It still didn't give him a clearer idea of her diagnosis, though in cases of schizophrenia, patients largely only seem to focus on the white space in between, rather than the blots themselves. All Pia seemed to be seeing was sex, violence and darkness. What the results revealed was that his patient was deeply disturbed, and it was unclear how many layers he'll need to peel through to get to the core. Luckily, though, Anando has found his way past the first. Though her response to every card was troublesome, it's the fourth and the seventh card that she reacted to most extremely.

Also respectively known as the Father card and the Mother card.

Pia

'But it wasn't my father I saw in the fourth card,' she points out the next day during their session.

'It doesn't have to be a paternal figure, though most subjects perceive it as male, and the reaction to it reveals one's attitude towards male figures. It could just be a symbol of authority, someone threatening, or perhaps, an indication of one's feelings of subservience.'

She nods, as if she agrees with the last part, but doesn't say anything.

'How did the card make you feel?' he prompts. He notices she is still wearing the same jeans and sweatshirt, with the edges of the sleeves worn down and frayed. Her hair is in disarray. It seems like she hasn't been sleeping much either. He makes a mental note to increase her dosage slightly.

'I felt like whatever was in it – it was going to hurt me … It brought back something … *things* … that I didn't want to remember.'

'Do you have a history of an authority figure getting violent with you?'

Pia immediately shakes her head, not wanting to open any kind of doors in her mind today. In fact, she isn't interested in telling him anything about her life.

He leans over, sensing this. 'Listen, I get it. You don't want to talk, but just know that – if and when you try to – I am not here to pass a judgement. I'm just here to ensure you get better, and for that I need your help.' Leaning back, he adds, 'I don't need to tell you what your answers on that test mean—'

'It's not a formal diagnosis,' Pia parrots him.

He smiles. 'It's certainly not. But maybe you need this more than you think you do. You're clearly struggling,' and this is a safe space.'

He starts to slam his notebook shut, like the session is over, and Pia realizes she isn't ready for it to be.

'Wait,' she says. 'It's my mother. I saw *her* in the card.'

He pauses, letting the book slide back open. 'Are you sure you want to talk about this now?'

She nods, and gulps down some air, before continuing, 'She used to hit me … when I was young. Her rage was so hard to contain sometimes, she'd go blind with it and hit me with whatever she could get her hands on – belts, shoes and rulers, or even hurl plates or glasses from across the room. And I remember never understanding what it is that I did to make her so mad. The reasons, even when I think of them now, seem inconsequential – left my shoes in the wrong place, didn't fold the laundry when she asked me to, or maybe because I hadn't got good enough grades in some test. It stopped when I was ten … maybe twelve?

'But before I could be relieved that it did, she started acting even stranger and scarier. She had these – well, episodes – when her rage would make her act possessed …'

Anando doesn't respond to any of this, keeping his face blank and letting her ramble. She prefers it this way, because suddenly she finds herself telling him things she has never told anyone else.

'The first incident occured when we were driving home from a PTA meeting. She was upset with me because my report card contained two Cs. She kept telling me how stupid I was. And how hard it was to love me. Then she pressed so hard on the accelerator, that we were almost flying. I remember opening my mouth to scream, but I couldn't. My voice was stuck somewhere inside me. And meanwhile, she just kept driving at breakneck speed, until she reached the very edge of the road, before slamming the brakes, while I sat next to her, thinking this was it. I am definitely going to die.'

Pia pauses, realizing she's shaking now.

'I was twelve.'

'The next day, she apologized. She said it wasn't her that did that. That she was … unwell.

'But then, a few months later, there was another such incident, where she kept banging her head against the wall when I didn't clean my room – telling me over and over again that I was useless.'

Pia recalls the heavy thudding sounds her mother's head made against the wall, as she repeatedly yelled at her to stop. She shudders as she remembers the skin on Neeta's forehead breaking, and the dark red blood staining the wall.

'Worse were the days when she wouldn't talk. Sometimes, those days turned into months of her sitting next to me, walking next to me, living right beside me, but not saying a word, because I had somehow upset her in some way again.'

Pia shudders now, thinking about those long periods of silence.

'How did you react to your mother during these episodes?'

'That's the thing – I *didn't*. I think my most immediate response was to hide in my room, with my paint supplies. Wait for it all to end. Because when it did, she would become the extreme opposite. Her guilt drove her to pamper me.'

Her mother would then take her to restaurants, where they would order truckloads of food ('let's ruin our diets!' she'd say excitedly), and power their way through it. Or she would get Pia to ditch school and they would stay in bed all day, watching *Seinfeld* re-runs on TV. Sometimes, she'd get them to dress up, and they would go out to museums and art galleries, and spend hours dissecting what they saw over fried chicken and sodas.

'She'd tell me then, "You know I don't mean that stuff, right? That it's just the anger talking?"

'And then she'd say, "You're my most precious, most favourite thing in this world!" And I'd forgive her. I'd even *forget*. Despite all of that, we were very close. A lot of people thought it was strange – the amount of time we spent together, the fact that we could bond like that, like best friends.'

But that didn't change the fact that Pia grew up with a fear of offending her mother in some way. She grew up trying to gauge her mother's moods from her voice every morning. Still buried deep in her bed covers, Pia would try to figure out how she was feeling from her tone and inflections and volume when she called out to the servants outside, before judging whether it was safe to venture out of her bedroom. Too loud – even if it wasn't directed at her, but at Raju – was never a good sign.

However, even if her mother was happy in the mornings, that didn't mean that the nights would be good as well.

And Pia learnt how to read the signs – oiled hair meant she was definitely depressed, Ghulam Ali playing in the background meant she was depressed and angry, sitting alone in the living room with a glass of vodka in her hand meant she was in the mood to be happy and mean.

'Happy and mean?' Anando repeats.

'It meant that it was best I didn't go anywhere near her, if I didn't want to be berated, or listen to jokes about my comically large nose, or how big my butt was growing. "I should open my own school uniform shop, with the way you keep outgrowing yours. Will save me money also or maybe buy a Domino's pizza outlet, to keep up with that growing appetite," she would say. I think it gave her some weird kick to be like that when she was high – which wasn't very often. I mean, she wasn't alcoholic or anything. I know now that she was probably going through some shit of her own. But … I don't know,' Pia shrugs.

Suddenly, she feels weird about betraying her mother

like this, out loud, in front of a stranger. But when she looks at Anando, she sees he gets it – how fucked up it really was. Pia realizes she's been waiting all these years for just that – for someone to get it.

'I remember her, literally emotionally torturing me in ways, playing these little games, toying with me. For example, she just stopped buying me new uniforms. Instead, the minute my skirts and shirts grew too tight, she would replace my breakfast with apples, and dinners with soup. I remember the fear that would grip me each time I saw a button close to ripping, each time the zip wouldn't go up. I am getting that weird metallic taste in my mouth just thinking about it, right now,' Pia says, looking away from Anando, and focusing on a spot on the wall above his head.

'Did you ever speak to someone about any of this? Your dad, or your previous psychiatrist?'

Pia sighs and shakes her head. 'No, I felt too guilty.' I felt terrible, as if it was all my fault and I had played some role in her becoming this way. I had no idea why I was constantly failing her. I reasoned that if I just locked myself in my room and didn't speak or move a single muscle, everything would be fine. But it wasn't the case. In fact, nothing I've ever done was right …' Pia notices she is crying, 'I would think in the back of my mind, she has never done this with Khushi.' Because there is nothing wrong with my sister. She is flawless. And I kept hoping that somehow, magically, I'd become like that as well.'

She reaches up to wipe away the tears and snot from her sweatshirt sleeve.

'Along with believing you deserved the abuse, did you also think that you didn't deserve her love or affection?' Anando asks her now, but the question confuses Pia.

'You don't understand, doc,' she tries to explain. 'I wasn't looking for her love or affection. In fact, she already loved me too much, and I was becoming choked by it. It was as if she was swallowing me whole. Unfortunately, I loved her in the same way. I mean, how could I not? She's all I've ever had.'

Anando

Is that where the demon originated from? Was it something that would free her from the clutches of the evil witch she saw in that card?

But how?

'So, what's the diagnosis?' Dr Khanna asks him, biting into an apple, as Anando scribbles furiously in his pad.

'I think it has something to do with the mother.'

The director actually laughs, then says, 'Well, it's always the mother.'

'True,' Anando says, trying to hide his disgust over the former's nonchalant attitude. 'This one's a textbook narcissist, also controlling, which explains a lot. In fact, I think I am seeing the outlines of Pia's demon now. She has clearly internalized all her mother's rejection and criticism, but she has also repressed aspects of herself that her mother didn't approve of – or that she was told were not acceptable. She is emotionally stifled. All that anger, anxiety and insecurity had to come out in some way, at some point.'

The director looks curious. 'Did she mention it then – the demon?'

'No. But I finally saw a hint of the Pia in the medical file. And I believe it's only a matter of time.'

Neeta

After telling Raju to wind up for the day, she goes up to her bedroom, locks the door shut and changes into her nightgown. She closes the curtains and switches off the lights before sitting down in complete darkness.

Then she allows herself to do something she hasn't done in years, or at least not since Pia was fourteen.

She lets herself go.

Ghulam Ali's voice fills the room as she nurses a glass of vodka in her hand, taking slow sips and savouring the high.

Dr Agarwal had advised against stopping the medication, but after Pia did what she did, Neeta had no choice. She had needed to maintain control.

'She's not your project, Neeta,' Dr Agarwal would tell her first. 'That's why you get irrationally angry when she makes mistakes. It's too much weight on her little shoulders. As a mother, you have far too many expectations of yourself. She doesn't have to be perfect. Neither do you.'

Yet, when Pia's demon appeared, Dr Agarwal began contradicting himself.

'You have to keep an eye on her at all times. Every move. You have to be alert,' he had said, after she told him about what Pia had done to Tuffy.

Despite telling her all along that Pia was not a project, that she shouldn't treat her like one, that she needed to let both her daughter and herself be – he was now telling her that she needed to do the opposite.

So, Neeta began focusing on her single-mindedly. There was no time to let go. To bother about her own self. In fact, she found that she was losing that self entirely now – she and her daughter were becoming enmeshed in her eyes.

That's where she had messed up, hadn't she?

How could she see a murderer in Pia when all she saw in that face was her own damn self?

How could she see Pia's madness, when she could feel she was losing her own mind too?

How could she have thought she could bring a normal child into this world when she was barely normal herself?

Instead, she had done the next best thing – tried to teach her daughter the art of faking normalcy. Giving her the map to fit in, in a world that wasn't built for them. That was why they couldn't fail – she had tried explaining to Dr Agarwal. Failing was not a choice for people like them.

'You should have said something,' Ajit had told her after he had realized what Pia had become, giving her a disappointed, dejected look.

And she had felt her violent anger return after years.

It's so easy to blame the mother now, isn't it? So easy to say, 'You shouldn't have done this alone.'

'Where were you all these years then?' she wanted to scream, as she felt his words slap her across the face and kick her in the gut.

That look was her worst fears realized.

It was him telling her after all these years, that she was unfit to be a mother after all.

Her stomach churned as the rest of what he was saying faded away. And all she heard in her head, over and over again, were the words: You failed. You failed. You failed.

18

Pia

'She couldn't have even told her friends and family where I am. My mother must have told them some shit like "Oh, she's doing a course on art curation in Amsterdam, or something equally pretentious",' she tells Anando in their next session.

'So, did you ever try to leave Delhi, and your mother?' he asks her. He doesn't usually like interrupting, or steering, patients. Instead, he follows their stream of consciousness wherever it leads them, but after last week's session, he can't help but wonder if the mother-daughter codependency was reciprocal.

Their relationship reminded him of Carl Jung's Mother Complex, which spoke about the neurotic effects of overly anxious mothers on their children. In fact, children with a Mother Complex frequently dreamt of their mothers as witches or terrifying animals.

According to Jung, the Mother Complex could lead to either an over-developed or stunted sexuality. Pia, he suspected, fell in the second category.

'Of course, I tried to leave at several points. That's what I resent her for the most – she wouldn't let me. She had her ways of making me stay. And she was good at it. She'd try and poison me against anyone who ever tried to get too close to me. And if that didn't work, she poisoned their ears.

'She watched me like a hawk the whole time. Checking my phone, opening my cupboards and going through my stuff, emptying my pockets, my bags and my diaries. She liked to call it "protecting me".'

Pia starts fidgeting with her sweatshirt again, as she continues, 'When I tried to apply to a college in Mumbai, because I needed to get away, she didn't speak to me for a month. She told me I was punishing her, that I was ungrateful and unloving. It didn't matter, though; in the end, the college retracted their admission offer, and I am pretty sure she had something to do with that as well.

'That's when I realized what she really wanted. That I wasn't allowed to be another person – a whole being, with an identity separate from hers. And I felt like I just wasn't strong enough to fight her.'

'I only managed to somehow break away at twenty-five – or that's what I thought at first. She got me my own apartment and told me I could start being free and independent. But after I moved out, I realized that nothing had really changed. She was still always present, ensuring I stay under her control. I suspect that she persuaded Dr Agarwal to prescribe me even stronger medication. She was well aware there was nothing wrong with me, really. Or at least that I wasn't what Dr Agarwal said I was …' Pia trails off.

'She started criticizing me even more after that. My weight, my job, my house, my life – she'd bitch constantly, relentlessly. Right up until last year, she was telling me that I won't be able to hold down my boyfriend, Raghav, if I continued to look and dress and behave like I did. Worst of all, she was always right. He was, technically, cheating on me. But I can't help but feel like she wanted him to. That, beneath all that concern, it gave her some sick joy to watch me fail at things. Because, if there was nowhere I could crawl to, if no one would have me, where else would I go but to her?'

Neeta

Her current persona, with all its cracks and splinters, was cultivated after she got married. Before that, she'd just been a small-town girl, born to Punjabi migrant parents in Agra. Her father worked as a cloth trader in the local market, while her mother slaved away at home. Their household was filled with so many children that their parents kept forgetting them at mandirs and markets.

They had real problems back then. They always seemed to be running out of food, clothes, space, and the air was always fraught with extreme tension.

That's why she couldn't tell anyone when it first started happening, because no one had the time to listen.

The moments when her brain went black – a wild, uncontrollable fire raging within her – leaving her drained, and sick and afraid.

Your anger sits on your nose, her mother would tell her,

dismissing her outbursts with a wave of her hand, too preoccupied with a new baby to nurse.

Neeta didn't have the vocabulary then, to express her fears, her anger or how she always felt like she was invisible. She was tired of fighting for space, things or even basic attention. Deep inside, Neeta knew she was better than this hovel. That she was meant for something bigger.

'That pretty face of yours has gone to your head, it seems,' her mother would tell her, when she tried to explain it to her. '*Par nikal aaye hain.*'

Ironically, Neeta had never realized how pretty she was until the world started pointing it out to her.

And when she *did* realize it, her first instinct was to get rid of it.

But no matter how short she cut her thick hair, it grew back within a month, with a bizarre vengeance, curling riotously, demanding attention. Her lips were pink and thick, and the kind that boys in the neighbourhood liked to call 'kissable'. Her large eyes, they would tell her, had a look that screamed innocence, but also whispered, 'come hither'.

That's probably why a stranger slipped her an application form for an Air India hostess job at the market one day. When she told her parents about it, they seethed and raged, and threatened to disown her if she ran away to become a '*hawaaii aayah*'.

She got the job and left that life behind her, watching with sick, perverse pleasure as her family and the rest of Agra grew smaller and smaller, turning into a tiny dot, before disappearing completely from her life.

The job lent her an exoticity and beauty that conformed to rigid discipline. And it practically gifted her a new version of herself. It was calming, almost therapeutic, for her to become that Neeta every day – draping that sari, painting on a new face, pinning and disciplining her hair back into a tight bun and speaking in an accent and voice that wasn't hers. The Neeta who could tell apart her cheeses and her wines, and Paris from Prague. The one who was nothing like what she had been in Agra. Presentation and grooming, she was told, was everything.

She realized now, the power that her looks held. How it swayed and manipulated men, but also made them crude and threatening. She was taught how to tightrope walk the line between alluring and aloof, and that lesson stayed with her – craftily applied later in life, be it while haggling with sabzi vendors or hosting dinners for bureaucrats at the Bhandari home.

At twenty, she met Ajit on a flight to New York. By the time they had landed, he'd asked her out on a date. By the end of their week-long stay there, they were married.

Neeta had a vague idea then that she was at the cusp of a brand-new life. That things were about to change in an even more significant way. When he first brought her home, she was shocked. She had never seen this kind of money before. There was almost too much of it, so much that they didn't know what to do with it. They ended up making ridiculous decisions like installing lavish Greek marble baths or insisting on eating oranges sourced from Australia. For the first time, she didn't have to be in survival mode. She could relax, preferably at the spa at the Taj. Well, at least for a while, before that old loneliness and hints of her dysfunctionality started creeping up again.

'Married-up' was a term she heard for the first time, when she attended a party with Ajit. She'd never heard it before, but she knew instinctively that those two women were talking about her. Despite her wearing one of her most expensive crepe saris to the event that night – they saw right through her. And why wouldn't they? She didn't know how to behave, sit or talk in front of his family and friends. And she had no real social skills, save for putting on an accent for a couple of hours, pouring out wine, and serving it with cheese and peanuts. None of which impressed these people because she wasn't from old money like them. She was a nobody – a flight attendant, which made her a cross between a whore and maid in their eyes.

Moreover, Ajit was a busy man, who more often than not, left her to be. She'd wander across the many rooms of their bungalow, trying to figure out what to do next as life continued to pass her by. Soon, she developed a new personality to help her cope – a new hair colour, a new makeup palette, a new voice, with a haughtier, grander tone to it. She managed the house like an orchestra conductor, presiding over the cooks, the cleaners and the drivers to create a harmonic routine. She managed to infiltrate the higher echelons of Delhi's society women. And all of that helped, for a while.

Until, just like that, one day, she stopped getting out of bed. When the days turned to weeks, and then a month, Ajit didn't know what to do, and so he called his sister Bubbly to speak sense into her.

'You've come a long way from your old life. Do you want to go back to struggling for the very basics?' she reasoned with Neeta, who shook her head.

'Do you miss being an air-hostess?'

No, she didn't. It had stopped being fun a while before she met Ajit. She was sick of men pinching her butt and cracking lewd jokes, of standing around in high heels for eight hours, of the constant taunts and of painting on a new face every single day.

But she didn't know how to explain to Bubbly that she had started feeling homesick – not for her family or that house in Agra. It was for something she couldn't name but knew she had never really had her whole life – a place where she felt like she truly belonged and people with whom she felt seen and understood.

'Do you think there ever will be a place where you will feel that way? Besides, I don't think any of us do. Neeta, you have everything in the world right now. You got lucky, darling. Women like you – no offence – I mean, women with no family, no money, with nothing at all, they disappear between the cracks. But you got your happy ending – a prince, this castle. Ajit is a kind man, and he has given you everything you could possibly need, and more. Now, stop throwing it all away.'

Neeta nodded through her stupor, finally seeing some sense in what Bubbly was saying.

'Also, you know the antidote for that loneliness, don't you?'

'What?'

'*Arre,* have a baby, of course!'

Anando

Pia stops fidgeting with her sleeves. He notices that she looks no worse than she did earlier today. He can tell she's getting used to the meds and her routine. To him. She's a lot more relaxed during their sessions. He doesn't have to prompt or cajole her to speak anymore.

'I think that's just our family dynamic – Khushi was daddy's girl, while I was my mother's. And Khushi and he were very close. They had their own secret language, with their little codes and shorthand. Even now, when Khushi's grown, they talk to each other in lawyer-speak over dinner, while mom and I just sit there, pretending to be interested.'

'Did you ever feel jealous of that?'

Pia shrugs. 'No, I felt … nothing. I didn't care. It's not like I wanted to be in Khushi's shoes.'

'And why is that?'

Pia sighs, 'My father is like folklore to me. All I know about him is what I've pieced together from observing his relationship with my mother, with Khushi, and what they have told me. I have no idea who he really is. He hasn't even come to see me here. He is keeping his distance as usual.'

'That has to hurt somewhere.'

'It doesn't.'

'You were in a girls' school and seemingly had no

relationship with your father. It seems like you didn't have any male figures in your life for a very long time. You think that hasn't affected your relationships with, and views on, other men?'

'Well, I had Dr Agarwal,' Pia says with a small smile. 'So, you can totally understand why I hate men …'

She acts like she's cracking a joke, but Anando's not quite sure that's what it is. In fact, she often acts like she's joking while inadvertently revealing new parts of herself.

'Do you really hate men?' he asks her now.

'I don't know,' she says, looking a bit uncomfortable. She's getting fidgety again, he notices. 'I certainly don't *love* them. They just feel like aliens to me, or another species.'

'And what about your boyfriend?'

'He was okay, aside from the cheating and stuff. He was …' She laughs. 'I don't know, actually. He minded his own business, I minded mine. It was a cool setup. It worked.'

Anando isn't surprised. People frequently seek partners similar to their parents. Even repeat unhealthy attachment patterns because it is what makes them feel most at ease. Pia sought someone who resembled the emotionally distant parent – her father. Which was understandable given her experiences and her mother's emotional demands. He can see why she would avoid intimacy.

'Plus, my parents liked him too. My mother *barely* put up a fight when I started dating him,' she adds, as an afterthought.

'Did you love him?'

'I don't think so.'

'But you were planning to marry him …'

Pia laughs again. 'Give me a break. Do you think my mother loved my absentee father? Or my sister loves her boring, equally absentee husband? That's what you do, man. You turn twenty-eight, find a mate who can support you, marry, and have a few babies before your eggs dry up.'

'Still, you must have had dreams of falling in love. Most women do …'

That causes her to pull her sleeves past the palms of her hands, gripping the edges with all her might.

'I just figured that stuff isn't for girls like me.'

'Why do you say that?'

She lets out another funny, involuntary, nervous laugh.

'Love is for girls who are attractive, skinny, mentally healthy. It was hard enough to get Raghav's attention, as it is. I wasn't going to pass up on a catch like that – chasing some vague idea of love, until my eggs dried up.'

'"Eggs drying up". "Catch like that". These sound like your mother's words, Pia. It's clear to see how much she harmed your self-worth. How adversely she affected your worldview.'

Pia clears her throat, before saying, 'I thought it was her instilling a sense of pragmatism in me.' She always did that. When he began attacking her mother, she defended her. Unlike other patients who sought his validation when they spoke about their abuser, Pia pretended like she was the only one allowed to say negative things about her mother. To others, Neeta was off-limits.

'Besides, imagine, if you'd never tasted chocolate, you wouldn't know what you were missing,' Pia is saying now.

'I don't know if I agree with that analogy. Our sexuality begins developing at adolescence, regardless of how we may feel about it, or however much we may deny it. Someone like Frued even believed our psychosexual development begins from birth. The very act of breastfeeding is sexual, according to him ...'

'Ewww, gross,' Pia groans. 'Please stop.'

He smiles, as he continues, 'Of course, that theory is widely contested.'

'I can see why ...' Pia rolls her eyes.

Anando continues, 'What I am trying to say here is, there's no way you hadn't had chocolate, you couldn't have not wanted it. Everyone does. It's natural, it's *healthy*. You must have had crushes growing up too. In fact,' and he says this very carefully, in an effort to not startle her with the D-word, 'Your demon appeared at an age Frued liked to call the Genital stage. It's supposed to be the time a person resolves all their psychosexual conflicts. For that, one also requires to be independent from their parents in some sense. But that never happened for you, did it?'

She already looks suspicious at the mention of the word 'demon'. She hasn't acknowledged it during therapy before, and Anando realizes this session could go either way.

There's a long pause, and he can practically hear the wheels turning in Pia's brain before she spits out—

'You think my demon was about *that*? My unresolved sexuality?'

She raises an eyebrow at him. She looks disappointed. Like she expected better from him. At the same time, he can see the relief in her eyes, now that it's finally out there. Her body language too seems relaxed, like she finally feels safe.

'Something changed during the summer you turned thirteen, isn't it? You were diagnosed with mental illness at a time when your body was undergoing massive transformation as well. It's a confusing time, physically, emotionally, mentally,' he tries to explain.

'Ugh. Stop!' Pia groans. 'Sorry to disappoint you, but it wasn't my blooming sexuality, doc. It was my friend, Ila. She was the one who introduced me to the damn demon.'

'How did she introduce you to this demon?' he says, mirroring her words.

'She was obsessed with the occult. Kept wanting to summon a demon, and one day she did. But instead of her, it ended up possessing me. The rest, as they say, is history.'

He can sense in her tone, that that's enough demon-talk for the day. And so he switches gears to, 'So, tell me. What was Ila like?'

Pia has a fond smile on her face, as she says, 'She was just the freest girl I had ever met. No inhibitions, whatsoever. She wasn't afraid of the nuns at school, or society, or, well, demons. I had never seen someone like her before. I mean, my mother hated her, naturally. She told me not to hang out with her or talk to her, because of how "loose" she was.'

Pia shakes her head, as if to clear her thoughts. 'But in retrospect, that was the one sane piece of advice my mom gave me. I should have listened,' she defends her mother again.

'And did your mother tell you why she considered Ila to be loose?' he prompts her, after she stops speaking.

'You know, she would go around with boys and stuff. She had a new boyfriend every week, in fact.'

Pia clears her throat, before saying, 'That was also the toughest part of being her friend. Being especially unattractive, they all treated me like some kind of a troll they needed to pass to get to her, you know? They'd approach me, all nervous and shifty and pasty, asking me to pass on messages and notes to her. That's when I really grew into my role of a sidekick.'

'It didn't make you resent her?'

'No, not at all,' she shakes her head wildly. 'I worshipped her!'

Anando doesn't buy it. Of course, Pia resented her. All of what she has said reflects a deep kind of resentment. But he can tell she's holding something else back as well. Something crucial that happened before the arrival of the demon, and he doesn't know how to steer her towards it.

She touches the topic on her own moments later, tentatively at first, 'Okay, maybe you are right. She made me think of, well, the chocolate – my sexuality – or whatever – in a way I hadn't before. I loved her, but there was a part of me that *was* jealous of the attention she always attracted – both, the good *and* the bad. It's like whatever she was, Madonna or whore, she was alive, visible and whole, in a way I had never been.

He sees the next words hit her like a revelation, as she says them out loud: 'And then one day, I walked in on her with this guy in her bedroom. It made my head flip. What they were doing … how comfortable she was … with being touched like that…

'I remember wanting that so desperately, but also knowing I never could. Those were experiences reserved for girls like Ila. And I would never be an Ila.'

Anando

'The demon first appeared at the same time as her pretty friend, Ila. In fact, she was the primary catalyst for it,' he tells the director later that evening.

'So?'

'In his essay on the Mother Complex, Jung had said that in cases where the daughter's Eros or sexuality remains under-developed, they consider themselves inferior to their 'superwoman', perfectionist mothers, ultimately rejecting everything feminine about themselves – be it in terms of personal relationships or sexuality. Instead the daughter chooses "to devote herself to her mother and live out a 'shadow' existence, sucked completely dry by the matriarch".'

The director still looks confused about where Anando is heading with this.

'That's what had happened with Pia too, I think.

The dependence was unquestionably reciprocal. She was choosing to reject her sexuality, to be sucked dry, and live out that shadow existence – until Ila opened up a portal to another kind of life, the one that Pia had been avoiding all along. Something Pia's unconscious started projecting, perhaps, as her 'demon'.

'When she saw Ila in that moment in her bedroom, Pia's already confused emotions surrounding her friend – resentment, jealousy, admiration and love – got even more jumbled up. Pia added that somewhere, she felt betrayed by her friend, with whom she had developed a similar codependent relationship, as with her mother. She told me: *'In that moment. I wasn't just jealous of Ila. I was jealous of the boy she was with too.'*

'Right,' the director says again. 'And several researches and case studies have shown women to channel their repressed feelings by believing they are possessed. They attribute their fears, anxieties – most of them latent – onto a higher or malevolent entity.'

'Exactly!' says Anando. 'That was the origins of this demon. In fact, I think that it was born in that precise moment in Pia's mind.'

'So, what do you think this demon really wanted from her?'

'That is what is confusing me. I'm not sure if Pia constructed her demon to break away from her mother or to help her become everything her mother wanted her to be.'

'You know, I've heard about these mother-daughter cases. One involves a twenty-year-old woman who developed total paraplegia on the morning of her graduation from US Navy training. All the tests, from MRIs to psychiatric evaluations, showed nothing. The doctors told her that there was nothing wrong with her, that her lower body was completely healthy. They determined the problem could be a disconnect between her voluntary motor centres in her brain and her leg muscles. Eventually, they discovered it was the pathological relationship between the mother and the daughter that caused the paralysis. The prospect of being transferred to distant duty had caused separation anxiety in the daughter.'

'How did they find out?'

'Oh, hypnosis and sodium pentothal. Under the influence, she got right up from her wheelchair and started walking. Told them all about her and her mother. You know the really messed-up part? Later, when she was shown a video of the session, the mother refused to accept that her daughter could walk. She kept insisting that she still needed the wheelchair.'

He realizes that Pia's equally torn about the demon's motivations too.

'Sometimes, it talks so much like my mother, I could swear it is her. Sometimes it is fun, but just as bossy as Ila,' she tells him.

When she describes in detail the day the demon possessed her, eventually convincing her to kill her dog, Anando isn't sure what to make of any of it.

He thinks about children who torture animals – playing out their future psychopathic tendencies, or perhaps dealing with the abuse they themselves may have faced in their lives, in the process, but Pia doesn't seem to fit into either of those categories.

Her mother forbade her from ever seeing Ila again after that. When Pia tried speaking to her friend, she was told that her mother had threatened to drown Ila and her family in lawsuits if she ever spoke about what happened or contacted her daughter.

Neeta got even more obsessive after that, Pia had said, making Anando wonder if that's what Pia had been unconsciously wanting all along. To perpetuate their co-dependent bond further, especially when confronted with the possibility – the threat – of an Ila? Perhaps, Pia even wanted to feel safer after the rejection she had thought she had faced, at the hands of men, as well as her only friend.

This theory is confirmed, when Pia starts talking about the demon resurfacing all those years later.

She says that it came back because she thought Khushi was sabotaging her by marrying before her, and because Raghav was cheating on her – choosing to mention this guy called Kabir almost as an after-thought.

It's a pretence Anando can clearly see through.

Furthermore, once she mentions his name, she can't stop talking about him, revealing herself entirely.

'Kabir was like a glitch in my universe,' she's telling him now. 'I just knew, after I met him, that nothing would ever be the same. He was the first person who truly liked and accepted me for who I was. People constantly tell me to lose weight, to behave in a certain way, to prove that I am, in some way, normal. Yet, Kabir treated me like I was better than that – like I was even special.'

'Why cheat on Raghav with him then? Why not date him instead?'

'Well, this is certainly not one of my proudest moments,' Pia says, fidgeting nervously, before taking a deep breath and letting it out along with her confession – 'I think I knew he just didn't fit in my world.'

Anando raises an eyebrow in question.

'He was ... how do I put this ... financially challenged?'

She almost makes him sound ill.

'I just didn't think that would endear him to my mother,' she confesses, and Anando finally understands what she means. 'Besides, I had worked really hard to get where I was with Raghav. It was all going smooth.'

'Pia, he was cheating on you.'

'Yes, but I ... I don't know how to explain it. I think I was trying to figure that part out, before the demon showed up.'

As it always does when Pia is confronted with real choices, thinks Anando. It showed up to remind her of the consequences her decision would hold – the biggest being her mother would never accept someone like Kabir.

Following its arrival, Pia says, it switched back and forth between Ila and her mother's voice – her latent desires mixing with what was expected of her.

It's clear that by this point, she had internalized Ila as another part of her personality. It boiled down to a single afternoon she had spotted her friend with a boy in her bedroom.

Kabir offered another chance for Pia to defy her mother and to come out from under her shadow. But she chose not to, again. Years and years of conditioning had ensured she never chose him, as it would be the ultimate failure in her mother's eyes.

Even so, the pressure valve had opened.

The volcano had erupted.

'In the months that followed, after the demon showed up for the second time, you became exactly what you had wanted to be. You looked like the ideal version of yourself, and you became a legitimate artist,' Anando says.

'Raghav proposed,' she points out, as though he had forgotten.

'And you think this was all the demon's doing?'

'It certainly wasn't a coincidence that everything started going right the moment it came back,' Pia says, with narrowed eyes, like she is challenging him to come up with a better explanation.

He gives it a shot: 'Or maybe, it could just be your unconscious – that repressed part of you living out its fantasies minus the conscious part controlling it. It feels to me like the demon almost gave you permission to act in any way you wanted. To become Ila or your mother, depending on how you look at it.

'It let you play out all your fantasies, conveniently shielding you from the guilt. It gave you the justification and encouragement you needed to keep meeting Kabir. And yet, it kept steering you towards what you already knew was your ultimate destiny – Raghav and marriage, and whatever else it is you think will make you feel loved and accepted by your mother.'

Pia sighs. 'Maybe, you're right about all of it. And

I've been playing along, because I'm sort of convinced you are too. But I still think there's one thing you're wrong about, doc.'

'What is that?'

'The demon's real,' she shrugs.

19

Neeta

'I don't think it's a good idea for you to see her right now,' Anando tells her, when she shows up at the hospital a few weeks later.

He refuses to let her past the reception.

Neeta's confused. 'But I am her mother,' she argues. 'Are you really going to keep a mother away from her own daughter?'

'This is what Pia wanted, Mrs Bhandari. Just for a little while,' Anando says, adding, 'It's been a rough few weeks. She has been dealing with some traumatic childhood memories ...'

Neeta looks at him with narrowed eyes, before realizing what he means.

So, this is how her daughter wants to play the game now. She is going to actually go ahead and play victim, after confessing to all those murders?

'Okay, I get it,' Neeta says, breathing in and out slowly, to keep herself in check. 'I wasn't the perfect mother. I had issues with my anger when Pia was younger. But I worked on those and I *loved* her, Anando. She can't punish me *now*, like *this*!'

'No one's punishing anyone,' Anando is saying calmly now. 'Perhaps we can reschedule a meeting for next month?'

It will be too late next month, she wants to tell him, but that would mean admitting to him everything her daughter has done.

Neeta tries to mirror his calm and rational tone, as she replies, 'You've known Pia for a while now, Anando. You know how sensitive and creative my daughter is. I was just trying to toughen her up. She was so naive – always making up these little stories in her head. Unable to cope with harsh realities. I had to help her fit in, in this world. I did what any mother would do!'

'I don't know about that. She's going through a hard time right now, processing all those things you did,' Anando says.

'Bullshit!' Neeta spits out, half-pleading. 'Listen, think what you may of me, but I really need to talk to her today. It's important.'

'Perhaps, another time,' says Anando, still polite, not realizing that it's his politeness – his calm and rational tone – that's pushing her further towards the edge.

It will be too late then! she wants to scream, instead saying in a restrained, measured voice, 'Something isn't right. My daughter isn't what I thought she was. She isn't what you think she is. She said something to me last time … and it's been haunting me.'

'What did she say?'

That she has killed more people, several more people. But Neeta couldn't dare say those words out loud.

Instead, she continues pleading, 'I can't tell you – not right now, not unless I speak to her first.'

'Mrs Bhandari, I am going to have to ask you to leave the premises now,' Anando says. She can read the last warning in it.

Neeta feels a black fog descend on her now, as everything goes a bit hazy.

She finds herself pushing past him, running down the corridor, in an effort to get to her daughter.

She dodges doctors and inmates, peeking through the holes in each door, while yelling out Pia's name.

However, it's not long before two attendants grab hold of her.

She submits to them, partly because she has no idea where Pia is anyway. On her way back to the reception, she sees the other patients peering at her through the sides of the corridor and those same holes in the doors with mild curiosity, as though welcoming their new housemate.

I am not one of you, she wants to scream, but she channels her rage at Anando instead.

'Has she told you? About what the demon does? How it asks her to kill people?' she's yelling now.

'What?' Anando looks confused.

He has no idea what he is dealing with, she realizes. Why! He's barely a child himself!

'That's how she thinks she gets what she wants. By *murdering* people. *That*'s why we put her in here, because she ran her car over someone on the street. She thought Raghav would propose to her if she did that,' Neeta laughs bitterly.

The attendants are still holding her, as she lunges towards him, trying to get closer in an effort to drive her point home. 'I saw that boy's body, Anando. It wasn't pretty. In fact, they told me she ran over him *twice*. I was a fool. I was trying to protect *her*. I didn't realize that it was too late. I'd already failed. That I had to protect the others from her.'

The two attendants are trying to escort her out now, which makes her regain her composure.

'Okay, fine, I'm leaving,' she says, wiggling and shrugging their hands off her.

When Anando motions for them to let her go, she adjusts her kurta and runs her hand through her blow-dried hair, the haughty expression he knows so well by now returning to her face.

'She's your problem now, but I have one piece of advice for you: Don't underestimate her demon, like I did.'

Anando

'Your mother came by yesterday,' he tells Pia during their next session.

He's still having trouble making sense of anything Neeta said to him, or the way she acted, like a woman slowly spiralling into madness. But he can't seem to shake off her warning to him.

'She must have not been happy to hear that I didn't want to see her,' Pia says.

'She wasn't.'

She studies his face for a long minute, her eyes narrowing. 'But she got to you, didn't she?'

He doesn't reply.

'I thought as much. I told you, doc, she doesn't let anyone come close to me,' she shrugs. 'What yarn did she spin this time? What outrageous methods did she apply now to misrepresent me?'

For a minute, he considers asking her what her mother meant by her accusations. Why she claimed her daughter had *killed* people. But he thinks better of it. Besides, Neeta had looked like she was five minutes away from being admitted here herself.

'Nothing. It doesn't matter,' says Anando, choosing to go with his gut instinct, which is saying to him now: *Pia isn't a murderer. She's just a confused girl.*

Also, her mother has destroyed her life enough, and he believes that Pia deserves the chance to get better.

Neeta

Ever since her turbulent encounter with Pia's doctor, she hasn't left her room. For the past week, she has been slowly making her way through the vodka bottle on her desk, with Ghulam Ali playing on loop in the background.

Ajit doesn't bother her anymore these days. Their marriage is over anyway.

As if it could have survived what Pia did, and the way she forced her husband to compromise his whole career to fix it.

So, she spends her days trying to figure out all the ways in which she failed, while replaying her daughter's words over and over again in her head: *I have killed more people. Many, many more.*

She started by searching for 'death' + 'construction site' on Google four days ago.

'Labourer found dead in under-construction Delhi building'.

The article was dated from a few months ago, around the same time she had first started noticing Pia's weight loss.

On Wednesday, at around 4 p.m., contractor Sumit Kolhi heard a noise and went outside the building to find Bhaskar lying right outside it, the police said.

With the help of a passer-by, Sumit took him to Deen Dayal Upadhyay Hospital where he was declared dead.

It said in the end that the contractor had been arrested for neglecting safety procedures.

Don't worry. I made it look like an accident, she recalled Pia's words.

She has been thinking about the night Pia and Raghav said they first met – at the opening of a club in Vasant Vihar. She remembers how, when her daughter brought him home – out of the blue, their story about how Raghav approached a 'stunning' Pia in a tight red dress, sounded strange to her.

To begin with, Pia didn't *own* a red dress at the time. Neeta knew the insides of her cupboard as well as her own, and she had never seen anything that wasn't black or loose in it. Neither was she the type to wear a dress like that. It had sounded to her like Raghav had been talking about an entirely different woman.

But that would be ridiculous, wouldn't it?

The expression on his face had made her uneasy too. The boy was in a trance, and completely smitten.

Neeta doesn't know what it is that she's searching for when she starts Googling clubs that opened in Vasant Vihar that year. She stumbles upon the Facebook page of one and starts scrolling down until she finds their launch party album.

It contains hundreds of pictures.

Pouring herself a stiff drink, she starts sifting through each. Half an hour later, she still hasn't found a single one of Raghav or Pia.

She closes the album in frustration, before opening it again, just to be sure.

This time, she starts looking at all the girls in red dresses, of which there are many. One, in particular, catches her attention. She's also been tagged in the picture. Neeta acts on her weird hunch, clicking on the girl's name and then copy-pasting it into Google.

Sure enough, the first result that pops up confirms her worst fear:

'Model Lavisha Anand found dead in a parking lot in Vasant Vihar.'

It says the body was found mauled, most probably by a wild animal. Her throat had been torn open, and her limbs ripped apart. There's an accompanying picture on the side too, proving it was the work of some kind of a monstrous beast.

With her heart now thudding and threatening to explode from her chest, Neeta goes through the album a third time, and finds what she was afraid of – a familiar shape lurking in the background of one of the photos featuring that girl. She zooms in to see her daughter standing there alone, unsmiling, in a loose black dress. Was it the flash that caused her eyes to appear yellow?

Or maybe it's finally time to admit that the demon exists? That she had known it was real all along?

She emails both the articles to Anando's official account, as well as another one titled: 'Reviled and Revered: India's bloodsucking demonesses.'

The email contains only one line: 'Ask her if she did it.'

Anando

He stares at the email.

Opening the links of the three articles she's sent him, he starts with the two about the dead people – except one was clearly an accident, and the second, an attack by a wild animal.

He then clicks on the one about demons. There's a graphic illustration of a 'Yakshini' – he remembers Pia mentioning this particular term while talking to him – which is almost caricature-ish in nature, with swollen lips and melon-like breasts and hips. In one of her hands, she holds the dismembered head of a man, blood dripping from it.

It has a Kalidas's *Shakuntala*-meets-Ramsay Brothers vibe to it.

Anando feels that the images of sculptures, rock carvings and figurines – found all over the country and dating back centuries, according to the captions – are a lot subtler.

The Yakshini is wearing something different in each of the sculptures and figurines, depending on where the artefact was found (up north, down south, or even in the western and eastern regions of the country), or which era it belongs to. Some have shown her bedecked in jewels, while others in nothing but a simple robe that's tantalizingly slipping off her body. The sheer polarizing effect of the Yakshini over the years can be seen in the fact that in some cave carvings she's shown in grotesquely contorted sexual poses and lording over orgies, while some of her idols – carved from marble and fully clothed in red bridal saris and glittering layers of jewellery – show her with that benign, sedate smile, just as saintly as any other goddess. While some rudimentary sculptures and carvings depict her clutching dismembered heads, other idols show her raising that same hand in blessing.

However, the similarity is striking in each of these renditions of the Yakshini – because the woman in them has the same smile, the same exaggerated curves, and the same eyes – often depicted large and pupil-less, with yellow stones.

In the article, Neeta has highlighted a few lines:

Yaksis (or yaksinis) are known to possess a malevolent and benevolent nature, and have been described as demonic in Vedic texts. Yet, they continued to be worshipped across India as goddesses of fertility, wisdom and success.

They are often depicted as beautiful, full-bodied seductresses, with narrow waists and large breasts, and are known to use their shape-shifting and illusion-wielding abilities to lure men into their trap.

Many texts detail how they feast on human blood, flesh and entrails.

They are also known to possess the forgotten women – the village widows, devadasis and whores.

Across India, they are worshipped for their abilities to grant wishes. However, some strictures warn that seeking a yaksi to grant your desires is inviting human suffering. All they do is feed those desires and create new ones, entrapping you in a circle of your wants.

In return for each of your wishes, they demand a sacrifice, with an ultimate aim of consuming your soul.

Confused, he shuts the email, wondering what to do about Neeta's deteriorating mental state.

He doesn't bring up any of it during his next session with Pia.

A week later, as he approaches the institute, he notices Neeta waiting for him at the steps.

'Mrs Bhandari,' he begins.

'I know, you think I am crazy,' she interrupts him right off the bat.

She doesn't look like herself anymore.

It's the hair that alarms him the most. It's no longer perfectly styled, which is extremely uncharacteristic for Neeta. It's in complete disarray, tumbling wildly down her shoulders, even as her kurta hangs off her slender frame, and her face is bare and wrinkled, revealing just how much she's aged in the last week.

In this untended state, she looks eerily like her daughter.

He can smell the vodka on her breath.

She's right. She seems to be in the throes of some kind of a breakdown herself.

'You need help, ma'am,' he tells her, as she approaches him. 'I'd be happy to recommend a doctor.'

'I don't need a bloody doctor!' she hisses at him, shoving a pen drive in his hand.

'You have to believe me. You have to ask her about those deaths. You are not safe. This *whole hospital* is in danger. Just … promise me, you'll take a look at what is in this,' she's saying now, so fast, her words get scrambled mid-sentence.

He nods.

She stands there, looking awkward and lost for a second before walking away from him and hurrying past the gate.

*

He's been playing the video on loop for two hours now.

Though the footage is hazy, he can clearly make out it's Pia who is driving the car. But he can't see her expression when she rams her car into a man walking down the street. The body flies a few feet in the air, before landing on the windshield, and rolling down the bonnet, crumpling into a heap at the wheel.

And just like Neeta had told him, Pia reverses the car and drives it over the body at a high speed a second time.

What the fuck?

It's hard to reconcile the image of Pia he has in his head with the cold-blooded killer in the video.

He reopens the article she had sent him last week.

In return for each of your wishes, they demand a sacrifice, with an ultimate aim of consuming your soul.

'That's how she thinks she gets what she wants. By murdering people,' he remembers Neeta telling him, a slow chill creeping down his spine.

All of a sudden, he realizes he doesn't know this Pia at all, or what she's capable of.

Pia

She can tell something isn't right during their next session.

For starters, Anando refuses to look at her.

'The demon, you said it was a Yakshini, didn't you?' he asks her, in a businesslike tone. 'The ones that are known to behead men, drink their blood, grant wishes …'

He never asks her questions usually. He prefers to let her choose what to talk about, patiently waiting as she arrives at her own conclusions.

'Yes,' Pia replies, uncertain about where this is heading.

'So, did she do that for you too? Grant wishes, in exchange for sacrifices?'

She remains silent.

'Why didn't you tell me about the accident, Pia?' he asks her.

Her heart sinks as she hears him utter those words. There's only one way he would know…

She chooses her next words carefully: 'Because of my mother. She *told* me not to reveal anything. I had wanted to, Anando. I was desperate to! But she said that … I would be sent to jail. And then she made me promise to not do it.'

He doesn't say anything. Pia can sense him withdrawing further. They'd developed a bond, or even a strange friendship, over the past few weeks. She'd felt safe with him, because whatever they'd had, it had been easy and comfortable, devoid of judgement. Now, the air between them feels cold, stiff and impersonal. Suddenly, she feels like a patient – the kind who needed shock therapies and to be locked up in padded rooms. At the same time, she feels vulnerable. She'd told him everything, and now he even knows the things she hadn't, thanks to her mother.

She feels it in her belly, the realization of a fear: that nothing good ever lasts. Certainly, not for her. Not if her mother can help it. The fear then turns into anger, as he goes on, 'How many other people have you killed, Pia?'

She leans back, knowing that whatever they had between them is over. All she can do now is stonewall him and her mother in the only way she knows how – by hiding behind her fortress of impenetrable expressions.

She watches Anando leave.

And just like that, Pia knows her mother has won again.

20

Neeta

'You don't look well …' Anando is now telling her.

Of course, she doesn't. She hasn't been to Yasmine in months. She hasn't washed her hair in two weeks, or waxed, or cut her nails. She can hardly find the energy to bathe these days, though she made a special exception for him today. Not only has she showered, but she's also changed out of her nightgown and into a peach salwar-kameez, though she finds herself drained already from all that activity.

She points to the sofa, as he walks into the living room, and clears off the mess on it – a forgotten typewriter, months-old laundry and ashtrays – to make room for him to sit.

'I am sorry. Domesticity wasn't Pia's forte,' Neeta tells him apologetically. 'To be honest, I just haven't had the energy since I moved in to clear up this mess. Besides, it reminds me of her, and after a while, it began feeling like I was surrounded by her,' she shrugs. 'I miss her.'

Anando stays quiet.

'Ajit and I are splitting up. It's … they think I am obsessed with Pia, and my conspiracy theories about her. They said I messed up by covering for her when she clearly killed that man. He and Khushi gave me an ultimatum: either leave my daughter behind at the institution and forget about her entirely, or to leave the house. This is what I chose,' Neeta shrugs.

Anando clears his throat, breaking her out of her self-pity trance for a few seconds. He looks so young, she notices. Almost like a little boy – dressed in a grey t-shirt and jeans, with his pretty, *pahaadi* features. She isn't sure why but she feels sorry for him, even though she knows he's met women like her before, who are on the brink of, she doesn't want to say 'breakdown', because that would make it too real.

'Are you speaking to Dr Agarwal? You really shouldn't be doing this alone,' he tells her now.

'There's no time,' she waves him off. 'You're in danger, you know that right? Everyone, *anyone* in her path is in danger. The demon … it's real, Anando, I've seen it. I just didn't want to say it out loud …'

'Let's not go that far right away,' Anando interrupts her, before continuing, 'After I saw the video you sent me, I went back to the articles. There's nothing to tie them to Pia.'

'She told me herself about the labourer,' Neeta tells him. 'She told me she had killed many people, Anando.'

'But how do you know that she actually did it. That she didn't imagine or hallucinate any of these things?' he asks.

'I feel like I've always known – somewhere deep down – that she was capable of these things, but I didn't want to confront it. The truth is, I didn't want to face it. So, I kept protecting her,' Neeta says, slowly feeling herself becoming hysterical, the panic building up inside her. 'It was *me*. *I* unleashed this monster into this world. There's blood not just on her hands, but also on mine!'

Again, the doctor interrupts her hysteria with a steady voice, 'She can't stay in the institute if the things you've said she's done are true. But before all of that, she must confess. And for that I'll need your help …'

Anando

Pia looks like her usual self, except happier, at ease, and completely off-guard. Exactly as he had wanted her to be, when he injected the sodium pentothal into her veins moments ago.

He sits across from her, speaking in gentle tones and sending her into a hypnotic trance, as he waits for the medication to take over. He switches on the video recorder on his desk.

It takes him a while to work her up to the point where he can hold up a picture of the dead model Neeta had sent him in front of her.

'Do you know this woman?'

Pia's swaying gently now, her hands absent-mindedly slipping into her hair, feeling its texture, as she lets out a soft giggle.

'You did this, didn't you?' he asks her.

She looks at him with an incomprehensible expression, before nodding slowly. She folds her hands and places them on the desk, resting her head on them.

He has to lean over and bend his neck to get to her eye-level that way, and feels a bit ridiculous in the position, as he asks her, 'Because you wanted Raghav? And the demon told you to kill this woman in exchange?'

'Bingo!' Pia replies, her voice sounding sluggish. Suddenly infused with energy, she sits up straighter, 'I did him a favour, ya' know?' she says, studying her fingernails. 'He always likes the young, skinny, pretty ones, you know, the airheads.'

Looking him in the eye, she continues, 'I mean, I know, feminism is about embracing all kinds of women. But like, they aren't just embracing oppression, they are falling down on their knees and sucking off patriarchy. It's degrading and demeaning for them, and also five steps back for the rest of us!'

Anando shows her the video of her hit-and-run.

'And why did you run over that man, Pia?' he asks.

She looks like she's trying to concentrate for a moment, before replying, 'To fix the mess I made that night, after lighting that bitch on fire – the one Raghav was cheating on me with.'

She leans over, before whispering to him, 'Guess what?'

'What?' he asks her.

'She was a young, skinny, pretty, airhead bitch too!' she says, before descending into giggles as though she may have just cracked the funniest joke in the world.

'The demon asked me to, in exchange for getting Raghav to propose to me, which he did by the way, like, five minutes later!'

She never really tires of mentioning Raghav's proposal to him, he notices wryly, before finally asking her his last question. 'Have you killed more people?'

'Oh, yes, many,' she replies, amidst fresh peals of laughter.

*

'You shouldn't have done that, doc,' she tells him the next day, when he plays out the tape to her.

She looks messy and hungover. Like she hasn't slept the whole night. She's managed to rip a hole into each of her sleeves, from where her thumbs peek out, wriggling nervously. Outside, the attendants had told him that she hadn't taken her meds today.

He tries to soften his tone, as he says, 'Your mother … she asked me to. She signed off on it. But you have to trust me when I say, I did this for you. To help you.'

She looks at him, with tears in her eyes.

'I feel *violated*. I feel *betrayed*. I fucking trusted you! You're the same as Dr Agarwal. You're the same as her.'

'This demon's the one that can't be trusted, Pia. It's going to destroy you.'

And he means it. He feels sorry for Pia, and this sickness that she's battling – the one he still doesn't have a name for. He knows it isn't the real Pia that committed those murders. If anything she poses a big threat to herself too. Deep down, he does have a soft spot for his patient and wishes he could have helped her more.

She looks up at him now with black anger in her eyes, but Anando's unfazed by it. Instead, he asks her, 'Do you know the state they had found you in? Before they admitted you to the hospital, and eventually brought you here?'

Pia shakes her head, looking away.

'It wasn't just that you were out of your mind, trying to kill your psychiatrist. When you reached the hospital, you were diagnosed with a severe case of anorexia nervosa. The doctors said that your organs were practically shutting down. That you had been minutes away from cardiac arrest either way. Trust me when I say this – the demon is not your friend, Pia. It was trying to kill you the whole time.'

Pia shakes her head again, as though rejecting his words.

'You know, according to Freud, our conscious brain is divided into three parts – the id, the super-ego and the ego.'

'I don't want to hear about more of that sicko's theories,' Pia groans.

'The id,' Anando continues over her protests, 'is the primal part of our brain. The part that's sexual, aggressive, even destructive. The part that wants what it wants.

'The super-ego is like our conscience, as well as our idealized version of ourself – or who we would like to be. It develops early in our lives, based on the messages and punishments we receive from our parents and the society around us that are supposed to help us decide what is good or bad behaviour, and what's acceptable and what's not.

'The ego, Freud said, is the part of the brain that is supposed to be more realistic than the other two. It's the part that handles the tussle between the reckless, impulsive id and the hyper-ethical super-ego.

'Now, there's no scientific evidence this theory is true. Actually, it's been mostly debunked over the years …'

'Then why are you telling me this,' Pia sighs.

'Because here's what I think. Your id is your demon, your super-ego your mother and your ego is you. What happens when you get possessed is that your ego disappears, leaving only your id and super-ego.

'The part of you that's realistic, rational, even self-protective, disappears. All that's left is this reckless, messed-up, self-destructive version of you, guided by your warped superego. Worse still, you have been most admired and celebrated when you were this version of your most conforming *and* your most destructive self. So much so, that in the end, you really started believing that 'eating' was worse than 'killing someone'. Being thin, being married to Raghav, being like Khushi, or Ila, or whatever else you think will bring you acceptance – it all took precedence over human lives. Am I making sense?'

'Barely,' Pia says, shutting her eyes as though in pain.

'We can't function without the ego, Pia. What do you think happens when you start appeasing your darkest, most primal, most aggressive side, without any guilt or remorse … just engaging in the single-minded pursuit of your goals?'

'I don't know,' Pia shrugs.

'Utter and complete chaos! You won't just end up

destroying other people, you will destroy yourself too. The id and the super-ego don't care what happens to you, and neither does your demon. It doesn't want to grant you your desires, Pia! If it had, it wouldn't have ruined you the way it did before you got here.'

'Maybe you're right, Anando. Hell, maybe Freud's right too!' Pia tells him. 'But here's the thing, I don't mind going down, as long as I take you all down with me.'

Something in her face makes him back away, as she says this. He hasn't seen an expression like this on it before.

'It's here, isn't it? The demon?' he asks her now.

Pia nods.

'What is it saying to you, Pia?'

For a moment he thinks he saw Pia's eyes change colour. But they're back to black now, as she says in a low, heavy voice that almost isn't hers – 'That she's fucking mad. And that you're *all* going to pay for this!'

*

He wakes up groggy the next morning, realizing he slept off in his office while still trying to research and come up with a diagnosis for Pia, as her past tests reveal nothing.

He knows that eventually he'll have to hand over the CCTV video to the police, and let them take over from there, but not having enough answers frustrates him.

He hears the director's footsteps approaching. 'Anando,' the director calls out.

'I'm afraid we can't keep Pia here any longer,' Anando

starts telling him, when he sees him approach the doorway, but pauses, as his eyes travel past the director's face to his broad chest and then his stomach.

'Fuck!' he yells, rushing over to the doctor, whose knees are now giving away, as he tries to walk into the office, clutching his own intestines, that are spilling out of his gut.

They seem to have been ripped out and chewed off by a wild animal.

'Somebody, I need help!' Anando screams, noticing for the first time, how eerily silent it is outside. The place feels like a ghost town. He looks at his watch, it's 11 a.m. *How can there be no humans in sight?*

He spots a figure approaching from the corner of the doorway, and the chilling sight freezes his blood.

It's Pia in her sweatshirt and jeans that were once blue but are now coloured in blood.

Her body is bent into a weird, unnatural posture – her back hunched over, her knees and her arms twisted in weird angles. Her gait looks inhuman too. As she comes closer, he sees the blood across her mouth, and the other half of Dr Khanna's intestines that she's swinging in her hand. She stops outside the doorway, looking at Anando with her head cocked to one side.

Her eyes, he notices, are a bright, burning yellow.

His heart stops beating, as he accepts that he's next. He closes his eyes waiting to be ripped and mauled apart, just like the director.

But then he hears a sudden groan from the other end of the corridor.

He opens his eyes to find Pia looking curiously in the direction of the sound as well. Seconds later, she breaks into a run. Anando rushes to the door of his office and watches as she bends down on all fours and flings herself onto the old, plump, grey-haired woman dressed in grey scrubs, gnawing at the side of her face, as her victim lets out loud, tortured wails. He can't look away from the strange, terrifying and absolutely revolting sight of human skin and muscle separating from the bone, as this creature rips the woman apart, bit by bit, with her teeth. Eventually, the woman stops screaming, her body convulsing before slumping lifelessly.

Pia gets up and spits out the woman's half-chewed-out ear. Then she runs past the other bodies littering the corridor, and out the main gate.

Anando surveys the scene around him: almost ten bodies, mauled, disfigured and ripped apart in the exact same way as the old woman. He seems to be the only one on this floor still standing.

Grabbing his stomach, he bends over, throwing up last night's dinner.

He knows it's too late for it in the day, but he finally believes her.

The demon is *fucking real.*

Neeta

Her daughter is embracing her.

You know I love you, right? You're my most favourite thing in the world, she is whispering in her ear.

Except this doesn't feel like a reunion at all; it feels like a goodbye. Pia caresses her face and Neeta hears her daughter's footsteps as she leaves.

Then Neeta wakes up. Disoriented, she first registers the glass of vodka on the bedside table.

And then she hears Ghulam Ali, still playing on loop.

Her eyes squint at the clock that reads 5 p.m.

However, this isn't her clock … or her bedroom. She almost panics, before realizing she is in Pia's bed.

Before she can sink into the sweet, black depression again, she hears the phone ringing over the ghazals.

Anando's name reflects across the screen.

'Switch on the TV,' he instructs her. 'They are just picking up the news … it's going to be all over the place soon.'

Still half-asleep and drunk, she starts hunting for the remote, finding it beneath a pile of clothes.

'What channel?' she asks disorientedly.

'Any news channel,' he snaps back.

Images from the hospital flash across the TV screen. Mauled bodies, blood splattered across the floor and the walls. The red ticker beneath reads: 'BREAKING NEWS: Carnage at Prarthana hospital; cannibal killer absconding.'

'Death toll: 15.'

On the side of the screen is a small box, with Pia's picture and her name underneath it. Neeta wonders if she's having some sort of a lucid nightmare, as she sits on the bed, staring at the TV, trying to make sense of the scene in front of her.

'Has she got in touch with you yet?' Anando's asking her now.

'No! How did this happen, Anando? Are *you* okay?'

'Yes, I am. The city is on red alert,' he replies. 'You have to wake up. We have to *fix this*.'

Still clutching the phone, Neeta stumbles to the bathroom. The sight that greets her there makes her let out a huge, piercing scream. Her heart stops beating for a few seconds. She feels her vision blur.

'Neeta, what's wrong? Are you okay? Talk to me …' Anando is saying on the other end of the line, but her senses are still in shock. She can barely register his words or what's in front of her.

Her eyes travel from the blood running across the bathroom tiles, to the bloody footprints on the floor and handprints on the wall, and then on the towel soaked in the same sickly maroon colour.

'She … she was … here, Anando,' Neeta stutters.

'What do you mean "was"? Neeta, are you sure she isn't there anymore?' Anando replies.

The thought that Pia could still be in here, in this house with her, makes Neeta's heart freeze in panic yet again. She gets up and locks the bathroom door shut. Stifling her sobs, and lowering her voice, she whispers, 'No, I am not sure. What do I do?'

'Where are you now?'

'In the bathroom. I've locked myself in,' she tells him.

'We are coming to get you, Neeta. Stay on the phone with me until then.'

Neeta realizes her white nightgown is covered in blood too. She remembers the dream, which wasn't a dream. Her daughter hugging her tightly. Saying I love you and goodbye at the same time.

Anando

At 8 p.m., his phone rings, a number he doesn't recognize blinking across the screen.

'You asked me what she looked like. You asked me what she sounded like. But you never asked me what she felt like.'

'How does she feel?'

'Sometimes, she makes me feel so good. Like a drug. Like how I imagine heroin would feel. Everything is a thousand times more colourful, more real, like all my senses are tuned to the world. I feel fucking alive. But then, the other times ...'

She trails off into silence.

'Have you heard of zombie ants, Anando? The ones whose brains are taken over by a mind-controlling fungus?' she finally asks him.

'No, Pia, enlighten me.'

'Every night, the ant, infected and invaded by this particular fungus, climbs to the tops of blades of grass instead of returning home with its fellow ants. It clings to that blade of grass with its jaws, waiting to be eaten by a grazing animal. If it doesn't get eaten, it climbs back down and returns the next night, and then the next. It keeps coming back, night after night after night, until it's finally eaten. All that so the parasite can produce more of its kind inside the mammal host that finally eats the ant.'

'Wow, that's fucked up.'

She laughs. 'I know.'

He laughs too.

Then, they fall silent again.

A few seconds later, she sighs, 'I can't believe I did that. To all those people. All those innocent lives, just *gone*. Because of *me*. I know I am self-destructing, Anando. But I just can't fucking stop and I am so *fucking scared*.'

She's crying now, but Anando doesn't know what to say to console her.

'I saw the demon, Pia. I never believed you before that, and I hate myself for it. I am so sorry. This is my fault too.'

'No, no it isn't. You *did* believe me. You did enough. Thanks to you, I know why it happened to me. Why it chose me.'

She's sobbing now, and it breaks his heart.

'What do you think I should do now, doc?'

'Is it there … with you?'

'Right in front of me. You know what's funny, it looks just like me. It's like that Rorschach card – the one with the two witches, staring at each other.'

'The Mother. You know, some people just see two normal, happy women in it too.'

She laughs.

'Where are you now, Pia?'

'Close by, somewhere. Don't worry though, I won't kill *you*. Not before Dr Agarwal, at least,' she says, cry-laughing at her own little joke.

'I'd really appreciate that,' he says, before growing serious, 'Turn yourself in to the police, Pia. I'll help you from there. We'll figure it out together – how to fix this.'

She doesn't respond.

'Don't do it, Pia. Whatever it is that it wants you to. The demon wants you to think you don't have a choice. It wants to take you to the point where you feel hopeless about coming back.'

'It's too late. The zombie ants, remember? Maybe it's good that I die.'

He clutches the phone harder, trying not to cry himself now.

'You don't deserve to die, Pia.' He realizes he means it.

'But who'll have me now? My mother? I am sure even she wants me dead. She's let me go. I can feel it.'

'*I* don't,' he says, through the lump in his throat. 'I want you alive.'

'No thanks, doc. I don't want to live my whole life sedated in a mental hospital with you either. I gotta go now. I just ... I guess I just wanted to say goodbye.'

But she doesn't hang up. She stays on the line, and so does he, savouring this last moment between them.

'Pia, what are you going to do?'

'It says it wants my soul.'

The line goes dead.

'We traced the number to a Salim Merchant,' a voice says from behind him.

He turns around to look at the inspector, currently hunched over a computer.

'She must have stolen the phone,' Anando replies, walking over to him.

'She's somewhere in East Delhi,' he's saying now, pointing to a blinking red dot on the screen.

'Why would she go to *East Delhi?*' Neeta says, scrunching her nose, as though she's encountered some kind of an unpleasant smell.

They had found her curled up in the bathroom, covered in blood and muttering senselessly. It had taken a while to get her out of the state. She had finally managed to shower and put on a white Lucknowi suit that struck Anando as both posh and funereal.

He's glad to see she's recovered ever since.

'To meet Kabir Mehra,' Anando replies. 'You think we can find his address?' he asks the cop.

Kabir answers the phone on the fifth ring.

'Kabir, this is Anando, Pia's psychiatrist. Listen, I don't have much time. I hope to God that you've seen the news. She's probably heading to your house right now. Whatever you do, don't let her in. I cannot stress this enough. She's very, very dangerous. And she'll do or say anything to get what she wants. Do not listen to her. *Do not* open the door!'

Anando cuts the line, staring out the window, as the police van weaves through the city traffic.

'Who is Kabir Mehra?' Neeta is asking him. 'Wait! Is this the boy from Khushi's cocktail?'

Kabir

He hangs up, clearing his throat nervously.

'Are we out of mixers?' Pia says from the kitchen. He goes over there to look at her but all he sees is her bum sticking out of the fridge. The rest of her is inside it, inspecting the contents.

He's still confused by her randomly showing up at his door, after ghosting him for the second time. He was going to slam it in her face, but she looked so much like she used to when they had first met, dressed in a baggy grey t-shirt and black jeans, her hair up in that will-fall-apart-any-second bun.

A hot mess.

He let her in mostly out of curiosity. *Mostly*. And she had insisted she fix him a drink before telling him where she'd been.

'No. Should I go and get some?' he says now, realizing that would be a great idea, considering what this Anando guy had just told him. Kabir recalls snippets of the exchange:

The news.

She's very, very dangerous.

She'll do or say anything to get what she wants.

What was the guy even talking about?

Pia wheels around, smiling at him. 'No, we'll just make them neat,' she shrugs, returning to the kitchen to find glasses.

Kabir grabs that opportunity to switch on the TV, putting it on mute.

He barely registers the bloody bodies, and the words 'Pia', 'cannibal', and 'massacre' on it, before the screen switches off.

Pia's standing in front of him, holding a drink in one hand and the remote control in the other.

'Why would you watch TV right now?' she asks him with a lazy smile on her face, as though they didn't see what was just on the TV screen.

In fact, what the fuck *did* they even just see on TV?

Was it the words 'Pia', 'cannibal' and 'massacre' in the same sentence?

It's all so ridiculous that his brain rejects the information almost instantly.

She places the drink and remote down, and steps forward. He lets her hold his face in her hands.

'I've missed you,' she says softly.

For the first time since she arrived at his doorstep, Kabir looks at her – *really* looks at her.

Her skin is a sickly translucent grey and he can clearly see the blue veins running beneath it. Her eyes are yellow too, with swollen red veins slashing through them; her pupils are completely dilated, and the expression in them is … *blank.* His eyes scan the rest of her body, and he realizes that it looks like it is rotting and decaying all over.

It hits him now, that the person standing in front of him isn't Pia.

And he doesn't know who the fuck this is – pretending to be her.

'I love you, Kabir,' Pia says, her face breaking into a grotesque smile, her eyes starting to burn yellow. 'I always have.'

21

Anando

With a pockmarked and weather-beaten face, a sprawling khaki-clad chest bedecked with all kinds of badges, the DCP looks like the kind of man who has seen his share of crime in his life. Yet, even he had to draw in a deep breath when he saw the CCTV footage of Pia's rampage at Prarthana.

'I've never seen anything like this before,' he'd told Anando, while they both stared at Pia breaking open the door of her room, grabbing the first attendant on the way and biting straight into his jugular. From there, she had attacked every single person on the way, leaving some injured and others for dead.

'What was she even suffering from?' the DCP had asked. Somehow, Anando had known that that wouldn't be the right time to say 'demonic possession'.

He was still struggling to come to terms with it himself.

It was particularly horrifying to watch her take down the director. The man was six feet tall and twice as broad as Pia who was a little over five feet. Yet, she had absolutely no trouble, jumping on top of him, knocking him to the ground, before tearing into his stomach with her bare hands and teeth, and pulling out his insides.

The sight of the large police team outside Kabir's building has already drawn a crowd. The constables swat at the curious onlookers with batons, to keep them from contaminating the crime scene.

'It's Kabir's hand that greeted us first,' the DCP tells him and Neeta, who are still in the police jeep parked a few metres away from the crime scene. 'It took us a good twenty minutes to find the rest of his body parts. His face was in the middle of the living room – and it is the only part of him she hasn't left a single scratch on.'

'Fucking hell,' Anando says.

An officer tells the DCP, 'We checked out the CCTV footage. She entered the society in an autorickshaw. Grey t-shirt, blue jeans and with her face covered. She left in different clothes. A maroon sweatshirt and black shorts. They probably belong to the victim.'

The DCP nods and barks a set of instructions to his team.

'You see that?' he asks Anando, holding up his phone. It's a picture of Kabir's dismembered leg. Pointing to the lacerations on his thigh,' the DCP adds. 'Teeth marks. She ripped him apart with her teeth. We have to save whoever she is heading for next, Dr Anando.'

Anando recalls his sessions with Pia and realizes: Raghav.

That was all she was concerned about towards the

end. The fact that he had proposed, that they might get engaged – her entire image of the idealized self boiling down to it.

In fact, that's the promise the demon must have lured her to kill Kabir with.

In return for each of your wishes, the yakshinis demand a sacrifice, with an ultimate aim of consuming your soul.

And he was sure Pia still hadn't realized that Kabir wasn't just a 'sacrifice'. That he was the ultimate bait, to claim her soul with.

Raghav

He finally remembers what happened that first night he met Pia.

It wasn't while dancing, like he'd thought.

He never bought her a drink, before using a cheesy pick-up line on her, even though – for some reason – he really thought he did.

What he remembers vividly now is the way Pia had crawled out of the shadows in that parking lot, in an ill-fitting red dress, her curves bulging and bursting out of it.

Her red lipstick was smudged and bleeding past her lips, or maybe it was actual blood?

He never got the chance to find out, before her mouth had clamped hungrily over his.

It all comes rushing back, as she gets ready to devour him once again.

He can smell her rotting breath, and feel the agony, as she bites into his neck.

Neeta

At dawn, just as the sky begins to change colours, she knows it is all over.

She feels a sharp stab of pain inside her, as though someone has cruelly yanked out the invisible umbilical cord that was still tying her to her daughter, and then everything goes dark.

All she can think about is when she first held Pia in her arms. How safe she had been, while tightly swaddled in a white blanket and clasped so close to her heart. 'She looks just like you, Neeta,' she remembers them all saying.

A part of Gurgaon's Golf Course Extension Road, where Raghav's high-rise building apartment is located is barricaded and swarming with men in khaki and bullet-proof vests, carrying walkie-talkies and loaded rifles. Numerous TV reporters and vans have all gathered a few miles away from them, where they wait with bated breath for their next piece of breaking news.

Neeta opens the door of the jeep and walks past them all. Ignoring their 'no's and 'please wait's and 'ma'am, you are not authorized to be here's. They can shoot her for all she cares. She's a woman with nothing left to lose.

'I need to go inside,' she tells the big, burly constable manning the elevator to Raghav's apartment. 'My daughter is in there. I need to see her.'

He ignores her, but she finds herself clutching his arm, digging her nails into it, crying, 'TELL THEM, I'M PIA BHANDARI'S MOTHER!'

'We can't let you in ma'am,' he replies, just as his

walkie-talkie crackles to life. For a moment, there's only static and then a voice says, 'We're bringing them down.'

'Please escort her out,' the constable barks at another khaki-clad man. A pair of hands grab Neeta, who refuses to budge.

Just then the lift doors open, and a body covered in a blood-stained white sheet is carried out. There's a groan, as the paramedic yells over it, 'The victim has lost too much blood.'

'Raghav,' she whispers.

'*Arre*, I told you to take her away!' the constable yells again, but the rest of what he's saying fades away, as another stretcher emerges from the lift.

Her heart threatens to jump out of her throat, and her knees buckle, as she recognizes the bare foot peeking out from under the white sheet.

'Is she … Is my daughter dead?' she screams at the attendant carrying her.

He doesn't reply. He doesn't need to.

Neeta feels the constable's thick, hairy hands pulling her away and, for a moment, she's almost thankful for it because she is terrified of what's under that sheet. Hideous scales or rotting skin, perhaps? A face to match the monster she knows her daughter had become?

And yet, seconds later, as though she has no other choice, Neeta lunges forward and rips the sheet off Pia. Gathering all her strength for their final goodbye, Neeta looks at her daughter for the last time and all she sees is her eyes, her nose, her lips – her very own face – staring back at her.

Acknowledgements

First and foremost, I'd like to thank Anish Chandy of Labyrinth Literary Agency for taking a chance on a first-time author, believing her story needed to be told, and ensuring that it was heard by the right people. Also, Anushree Majumdar, who pushed me to get this book where it needed to go.

I couldn't have asked for a gentler and more encouraging editor than Isha Banerji at Pan Macmillan India. Thank you for 'getting' Pia, for being just as excited about her and for making *Batshit* so much better. Another big thank you to Pia Alizé Hazarika for the brilliant cover illustration.

I would have put off writing this book for decades if it hadn't been for my mother Rozita Kapoor, who simply replied, 'Then write another one,' when I complained, 'But what if it's terrible?' and my father Anil Kapoor, who has always pushed me to jump and reminded me that he's here to break my fall.

Here's just one of the many, many thanks I owe to Anshul Chaturvedi for always encouraging me to write, for believing I could be an 8/10 even when I thought I was a 4 and for opening so many doors in my life.

I am so very grateful to the three greatest loves of my life who suffered through endless drafts and rants about Pia's (as well as my own) demons:

Apoorva Dutt, my best friend and hype-woman, who virtually held my hand the entire trip from Mumbai/ Singapore/London. It only strengthened our twisted, co-dependent bond.

Kashika Saxena, my bro from Jaipur/Mumbai/Gurgaon, who dropped everything to send me her exclamation-marked, all-caps feedback that meant EVERYTHING!

Shwetank Powar, my husband, for letting me eat his brain for plot points and titles and for the constant reminders to breathe … and bathe … when it all got a little too overwhelming.

Writing a book can be a deeply lonely process, as well as an exercise in self-doubt, so I'd like to give a shout-out to my cats, Gundi, Mao and Phoolan, for their 4 a.m. cuddles, which helped me power through both.